Truth at Gunpoint

Truth at Gunpoint

Ray Hogan

SAGEBRUSH
Large Print Westerns

First published in Great Britain by ISIS Publishing Ltd.
First published in the United States by Five Star Westerns

Published in Large Print 2006 by ISIS Publishing Ltd.,
7 Centremead, Osney Mead, Oxford OX2 0ES
United Kingdom
by arrangement with
Golden West Literary Agency

British Library Cataloguing in Publication Data
Hogan, Ray, 1908–
    Truth at gunpoint. – Large print ed. –
    (Sagebrush western series)
    1. Western stories
    2. Large type books
    I. Title
    813.5'4 [F]

ISBN 0–7531–7556–8 (hb)

Printed and bound in Great Britain by
T. J. International Ltd., Padstow, Cornwall

Contents

Foreword

by

Gwynn Hogan Henline

It has been said that Ray Hogan's books are timeless, and with the passing of time books he wrote half a century ago read as fresh and exciting as they did when he wrote them. Why? Probably because he had that particular genius for being able to think up fresh and exciting plots and because he adhered to the cowboy code. This is a code that stressed fairness, morality, love of this great country and its laws, and love of all people.

As a very young boy, Ray watched the law at work, his father Tom Hogan being a sheriff in Willow Springs, Missouri before moving his family to Albuquerque, New Mexico. Tom further pursued his law career by becoming a member of the Albuquerque Police Force.

Armed with an insatiable thirst for Western knowledge, Ray spent much time in research and traveled thousands of miles to enhance his knowledge of the Old West with his wife Lois by his side. She was an artist and dress designer and did much of her designing while "riding shotgun" on their trips over the years.

Ray's writing ability was evident early in his life, in short, short stories written as assignments in grade school and junior high. He graduated from Albuquerque High School in 1927, with the following listed under his picture: Latin Club '26, Record Staff '26, Literary Emblem '27, Correspondence Club '27, Correspondence Club Pageant '27, *Bullet* '27. He married Lois the August after graduation and went to work for his older brother Archie, who owned a bakery. He was writing fishing and hunting stories at that time, something he continued doing while my brother and I were growing up. One of the things we remember about our young years was waking up at night and hearing the gentle clacking of his typewriter as he created a new story, then it was back to his daytime job the next morning.

There were few if any places in New Mexico and Colorado that my mother, my brother, my dad, and I didn't fish or hunt every spring, summer, and fall on weekends. There's a lake called Bluewater near Gallup, New Mexico that was one of our favorite haunts. The four of us spending the night in our Buick Roadmaster (one of those with only two jump seats in the back) because a family of skunks took over our tent for the night is a memory that has fragrantly lingered with us over the years.

As children, my brother and I were taught by our dad how to handle firearms; he taught us how to fish, how to hunt, and taught us to respect and love the outdoors, a fact that is very evident in his vivid descriptions of the areas where his stories take place. Reading his books again today, I know exactly what his main characters are because his descriptions are so accurate. You might say those were so-called trademarks of his stories. His locations and the depth with which he developed his characters blended in with such care and passion that you, as the reader, became another one of the characters. In doing this, you are able to enjoy the beauty of our West and endure the trials and tribulations right along with the others sharing that story with you.

With my brother and me grown, Ray decided to write full time in the 1950s. After a couple of false starts, he settled down into what was to be his routine for the rest of his life. He would go into his study at eight in the morning, work for a couple of hours, take a coffee break, then return and work until lunch. Back at work, coffee break around three, then write until 5:00p.m. Ray loved his coffee. Lois never acquired a taste for it, but back about 1972 she determined that she would share his coffee breaks with him and she did. Her coffee cup was about one-half coffee, one quarter milk, and many teaspoons of sugar. How she downed that concoction we'll never know, but until Ray died, she "enjoyed" her coffee break with him.

Lois proofread every one of Ray's manuscripts and was his severest critic. She never hesitated to tell him if there was something about the plot, a character, whatever she did not like, and, according to him, every time he would pull back, think it through again, and always ended up reworking it. She was never wrong, he would tell you proudly.

The women in Ray's books all had something of Lois in them. Whether it was the physical appearance, her beautiful, long black hair, her startling blue eyes, the sprinkle of freckles across her nose, her petite, lithe figure, or her ability to handle a needle as well as a pistol or rifle: these attributes were all Lois. There are women with her bulldog determination, an unflagging devotion to their man, a sense of humor and mischief, and the occasional, yet memorable, flare of anger.

I don't know how it is with the families of other writers; it was rather interesting being around him on family occasions. If he was writing a book, he was there, but he wasn't. We soon learned not to get upset if that faraway look in his eye was present. There was one family Thanksgiving I especially recall. He was called "Papa" by his grandchildren and great-grandchildren. He was mentally working through some point in his current book while I watched. A great-grandchild (ten years old at the time) walked up to him as he was seated at the dining room table and asked: "Who are you talking to, Papa?" He smiled, put his arm around her shoulders, kissed her on the forehead, and said: "Oh, it's someone I don't think you know. A man named John Rye." She thought about it for a minute, then her face lit up and she said: "Isn't he the doomsday man?" Somewhat taken aback he asked her: "How do you know that name?" She replied: "I heard my daddy telling his friend about him and thought it was such a funny-sounding name!" There was a wry pride in his smile that particular day!

When Ray wrote series books about Colonel Mosby, Shawn Starbuck, and the Doomsday Marshal, you came away with the satisfaction of knowing that the purpose that drove each of these men would be finally resolved. He didn't leave you hanging out there on that chance that he might write another one. When he started a series, he knew exactly how many stories he was going to write and how it was going to end before he typed the first word of the first story.

As his daughter, I have never decided whether he was a "wanna-be" cowboy or had actually been one in a past life. Back in the 1970s we had a friend who was a French teacher at a high school in Albuquerque who used Ray's Colonel Mosby series, which had been printed in French, as a teaching text for his French class. The children of those students are, today, reading the same Ray Hogan stories and enjoying them as much as their parents did. We are so fortunate that he chose to share his remarkable talent with us and the rest of the world.

I didn't inherit any art ability from my mom — that went to my brother Mike — so I figured that I would probably have the writing gene from my dad. After all, I had written several things for school magazines that had been published. Writing longer things shouldn't be any problem. I listened intently as my dad patiently explained what worked for him but brushed off his warning that these things would not necessarily work for me. As the saying goes, the acorn does not fall far from the tree. Right!!! I labored for the better part of three years trying to write good fiction, trying to talk myself into thinking I was enjoying it. Rejection slips became an important part of my lifestyle in those years. Then my husband, small daughter, and I moved to

Muskogee, Oklahoma and I found myself in the midst of a different Native American culture. I gave up writing and devoted my time to research and realized this was something I was really enjoying doing. I made copies of my information and sent it to my dad, and even today, as I re-read his books, I come across items that I had sent him from my research. There were some very interesting facts about the surrender of the Apache chieftain, Gerónimo, and I pointed them out to my dad. Neither one of us had been aware that he had surrendered in Arizona. The more we talked, the more excited I got about the information, and I asked him if he felt we could write a story together about Gerónimo.

We collaborated on "Bitter Sunset". I wrote the rough draft. He showed me how to develop a theme and how to develop characters, and I must say it was fun and so satisfying. I realized, when we finished the story, that I was not a fiction writer, while I did enjoy research and did enjoy writing factual articles. He put me in touch with the editors of the New Mexico magazine and Sun Trails magazine, and I spent the next five years writing historical articles with a detour into humor occasionally. He was always so supportive and exactly what you might think a writer father should be.

Although troubled by eye problems in his later years, Ray continued to put in several hours a day writing. We have found several legal pads with ideas, scenarios, and characters listed that he was working on. My husband Scott and I gave him a personal computer in hopes it would make it easier for him to see to write about a year before his death. Scott spent three days explaining to him how to use it as a word processor. The next time we went up, he had moved it to the other side of his study. The next time it was in another room, and finally it ended up in the basement. He had one way of writing: first it was handwritten on a legal pad, then it was typed and he hand-corrected it. It was then typed again, and the process was repeated until he had the final draft. The one adaptation he did make was to graduate from the manual typewriter to an electric one. How many electric ones he wore out, I have not a clue.

Ray Hogan may be gone from this life, but his words live on, and every time we pick up one of his books and become a part of that particular story, we ensure the fact that he will live on forever.

Ben Sutton's Law

Ben Sutton rode into Mexican Springs around noon. He was worn, dusty, out of sorts, and there was blood on his neck as the result of an attempted ambush in rugged Navajo Cañon. Now, as he turned into the deserted street, a taut anger glowing within him, he sent his hard gaze sweeping back and forth, probing like a piercing shaft of light the passages between buildings, doorways, and windows — even the low roofs of the sun-grayed structures. They had tried to kill him once that day. No doubt they'd try again.

No one was in sight at that blisteringly hot hour, everyone apparently electing to stay well under cover for reasons of comfort, but he knew he was being watched — had been, in fact, since that moment when he had ridden out of Santa Fé. He had thought possibly the news of his mission north had been leaked, and it was still a possibility, but he gave credibility to the idea that it was some of the Denison gang, the few remaining after his encounter with them near Magdalena. They had sworn revenge and they were the sort who would never give it up.

That they were the ones who lay in wait for him in the cañon north of Taos seemed the most likely, and

1

only that instinctive presage of danger, so thoroughly instilled in him by numberless encounters with danger, had kept him alive in those flaming moments, for small flags of warning had begun to wave inside him shortly after he forded the Río Grande and was moving onto the flat that separated the river from the black-rocked slope of the cañon to the east. Thus he had been more than half ready when the attack came. He had downed one of the four, but the others had escaped without affording him a chance to identify any of them.

His eyes picked up no suspicious movements along the way, and spotting a livery barn across the front on which the sign **O'HARA'S STABLE — HORSES TO RENT** was boldly lettered, he angled toward it, taking note as he did of its proximity to the Chama Hotel. At the stable he swung off stiffly, and handed the hostler the reins.

"Feed him good . . . and rub him down. He's had a long day."

"Yes, sir . . . it'll be a dollar," the hostler replied, and spat brown juice into a nearby corner.

Sutton laid the coin in his hand, dropped back to the board sidewalk, and made his way to the hotel. As he crossed the porch, a man swung into the street at its far end. The rider was entering the settlement from the north, the direction opposite to that followed by him, but he slowed, nevertheless, the natural caution in him insisting that he take notice.

Standing just within the Chama's entrance, he watched the horseman pull up to O'Hara's, stop. Dismounting, he entered the sprawling building. He was gone for only two or three minutes, and then returned, swung to his saddle. Glancing down the street, he wheeled around, rode back out of town, doubling over his own tracks.

Stiff, wondering, not fully satisfied, and with tension still drawing his nerves to wire tautness, Ben Sutton moved on into the shadow-filled lobby of the hotel and walked to the desk, ignoring the three or four loungers seated in the deep chairs and the solitary customer eating a midday meal in the adjoining dining area.

"Hot day," the clerk observed hopefully. He had a round face, unblinking, watery eyes, and there wasn't much hair left between him and heaven. "Come far?"

Sutton took the small pencil handed to him and bent over the register. "Not far," he murmured.

He received his key, listened to the room's number, and settled his glance on the man. He had a direct, disturbing way of looking at a person, and the clerk shifted nervously.

"Know a man around here named Whitcomb?"

The man brushed at his balding pate. "Sure . . . yes, sir. Everybody knows Amos. You looking for him?"

Ben said — "Could be." — and hesitated, his gaze settling on a girl coming through the doorway. He watched her approach, having a man's normal appreciation of her dark eyes, chestnut hair, well-developed beauty. She stopped at the desk.

"Tom . . . have you seen Yancey?"

The clerk frowned, pursed his lips. "Sure haven't. Ain't seen him for several days, in fact."

She turned away, murmuring: "He was home last night, but now . . ." Her words broke off suddenly as she saw Sutton close by. A flush mounted her face. "I . . . I'm sorry! I didn't mean to interrupt . . ."

"No harm done, Miss . . . Miss . . . ?"

"Murdock . . . Martha Murdock," she supplied.

He removed his hat, inclined his head courteously. "My pleasure . . . Ben Sutton . . . at your service, ma'am."

She smiled and for an instant the worry in her eyes faded, and then, nodding, she wheeled about and returned to the sidewalk.

"That brother of hers," the clerk said, wagging his head, "he sure does worry her aplenty."

Interest stirred along different lines within Ben Sutton as he made the connection of names — Murdock, Yancey Murdock. That had meaning and his thoughts went to the packet of letters inside his shirt that contained also special authority granted to him by the territorial governor. The girl's face blurred, receded into the background just as had other personal considerations in the time gone. To Ben Sutton the law, as always, came before all else.

"You want me to send the swamper after Whitcomb?"

He shook his head at the clerk's offer, turned, and made his way to his quarters — no better, no worse than the hundreds of other hotel rooms he'd tenanted during his life. After stripping down, he washed himself with the tepid water standing in a china pitcher, using the bowl that complemented it, then, propping back the dusty curtains in the hope of finding a vagrant breeze, he stretched out on the creaky bed for a nap.

He awoke shortly after sundown, feeling much better, dressed, and went into the dining room. A half dozen patrons were there, and, touching each with a close glance, he selected a table in a corner where he had a wall to his shoulders and a complete view of the room to the front. He ordered a meal.

Half through its completion he saw an elderly man enter from the hotel's lobby, after having first paused for brief words with the clerk, and move toward him. He drew up before the table.

"You Sutton?" He had a raspy sort of voice and a nervous habit of clenching and releasing his fists as though exercising his fingers.

Ben completed the swallow of coffee he had just taken, said: "Expect the clerk told you that. Would you be Amos Whitcomb?"

"That's me," the older man said, drawing out a chair and sitting down. Raising a hand, he motioned to the waitress for a cup of coffee, noting at that moment the welt left by the bushwhacker's bullet on Sutton's neck. "You had trouble getting here, I'd say."

"Some," the tall rider replied, sizing up Whitcomb through partly closed eyes. He recalled the governor's words: long-time settler in the area, owns the general store, has a finger in the bank, generally runs things in that part of the country. That struck him as being a bit odd; if Whitcomb was such a power, why did he go to the governor for help?

"Expected you yesterday . . ."

"Late start," Sutton said. "And that ride's no Sunday picnic."

"For a fact. Howsomever, no harm done. You're here in time."

"So?"

"Word's going around . . . there'll be a raid tonight."

Ben Sutton's eyes were on the window, on three vague shadows beyond in the darkness of the street. They could be the surviving three from his encounter in Navajo Cañon just as the man he had seen ride up to O'Hara's stable might have been one of them, but he had been given no good look at any of them and so could not be sure.

"Vigilantes?"

Amos Whitcomb nodded. "Justice Committee, they call themselves. There's a homesteader upcountry a few miles. Been some beef turning up missing. They're blaming him."

"Do you?" Sutton asked, letting his eyes strike fully at the man.

Whitcomb shrugged. "Don't rightly know. Reckon you could even say I doubt it. But somebody's doing it, and there's them that's got their minds made up. Point is, what can you do about it?"

Ben settled back in his chair, threw his glance again to the street beyond the window as he fished his sack of makings out of a pocket. The three men were gone.

"My job to do something, for sure," he said, starting a cigarette. "Not certain yet just what. This homesteader . . . what's his name and how'll I find his place?"

"Bovey. Follow the river north to the buttes. You'll run right into it."

Sutton sucked his smoke into life, shook out the match, and tucked it into his vest pocket. "You still of an idea that Yancey Murdock is the head of this Justice Committee?"

Alarm spread quickly across Whitcomb's features. He glanced hurriedly about the room. "Now, I didn't say exactly that. Said it was a rumor . . . only maybe . . ."

"I see," Ben murmured. It was always the same — a man wanting a disagreeable job done but desiring no part of it himself. He guessed he'd never get used to it.

"What about your town marshal? Won't he take a hand in things?"

"Gilcrist? Don't expect nothing from him. Old . . . about all he's good for is to run in the Saturday night drunks."

"Represents the law . . . ought to mean something. If he can't do that, best you make a change."

"Nobody wants the job . . . leastwise until we can sort of settle things down, nobody does."

The moments ran on, hushed yet filled with the faint rattle of pans in the restaurant's kitchen, the drone of conversation in the hotel's lobby, the slow beat of a horse's hoofs as it passed along the street. Somewhere off in the distance a church bell was tolling, summoning the faithful.

Whitcomb shifted in his chair. "Care to let me in on what you're aiming to do?"

Sutton's answer was flat. "No . . . it's a one-man circus, best to keep it that way." He paused, said: "One

7

thing, anybody here know you wrote the governor asking for me?"

"No, sir . . . nobody!" the merchant exclaimed, his face coloring indignantly. "You think I . . . ?"

"Not thinking anything special," Sutton broke in. "Just wondering about things."

Whitcomb shrugged, got to his feet. He brushed at the sweat on his cheeks, shoved his chair back into place. "You want me, you know where I'll be . . . my store," he said and, turning on his heel, cut back through the hotel lobby.

A bit later Ben saw him come into the street, bend his steps for the wide, long, running porch that fronted his establishment. Amos Whitcomb was a man not too difficult to understand; he was simply looking out for his own best interests.

The merchant disappeared in the blackness of his building, and almost immediately Ben saw a man come from the marshal's office, cross the street at a leisurely pace. He was well up in years, his trailing mustache and shoulder-length hair now a snow white, but he carried himself erectly, as if wanting one and all to see the star he wore pinned to the pocket of his vest. He'd been the town's marshal for twenty years or more — and his time was past but it was not in the man ever to admit it.

A stir of pride moved through Ben Sutton, as it always did when he encountered one of the old lawmen still going about his task. These were the fellows all settlements were indebted to, for they were the ones who laid their lives on the line every hour of the day and night just so a man and his wife could walk down a street, or their children could go safely to school. But only too often, as the case appeared here, they were forgotten, relegated, as an old horse might be, to the pasture of meaningless, harmless chores.

He watched Gilcrist come through the doorway, make his survey of the now almost empty dining room, and then move up to his table and halt. Despite the heat, the lawman wore his shirt sleeves cuffed and a string tie closing the collar.

"'Evening," he said. "Don't recollect seeing you around before."

"Rode in about noon," Sutton replied agreeably.

He was studying the marshal, not sure if this was the usual, casual inquiry of a town's lawman checking on a new arrival, or if it went further than that. Gilcrist could have seen him in the café with Whitcomb, was now on a fishing expedition, or his appearance shortly after the merchant had departed could be just coincidence. He wished he could invite the man to sit down, talk things over with him, ask a few questions that he needed answering — but that was out. A man doing the job assigned to him must necessarily work alone. To ask one question of an outsider that related to the matter under attention might arouse suspicion and undo weeks, even months, of hard work. That was one of the things that all too often disheartened Ben Sutton — that eternal, lone-wolf way of life.

"Aim to be around long?"

"Hard to say, Marshal."

Gilcrist drew out a bandanna, mopped at his craggy features. "Just one thing I've got to say . . . I'm running a peaceful town. Want to keep it that way. You got other ideas, you'd best mount up and ride on."

"You'll get no trouble from me," Ben said. "Seems I've heard other things about your town, though . . . about how . . ."

"You're talking about what's going on in the valley. Got nothing to do with my town."

Words to the contrary came swiftly to Sutton's lips, but he held them back. It was pointless to get in an argument with Gilcrist who seemed determined simply to turn his back on everything outside the town's limits — and there was that danger of tipping his own hand, arousing suspicion that could cause complications.

"Glad to hear that, Marshal," he said, rising and dropping some coins on the table to pay for his meal. "Town's quiet . . . always a good sign."

Lon Gilcrist bobbed his head, smiled briefly, and turned away. Sutton watched him leave, and, when the lawman was again visible in the street, he moved back into the lobby and went to his room. He stood by the window for a full hour, gazed on the street, wondering about the three men he had noticed, and then quietly left his quarters, followed out the hall to the rear door, and let himself into the alley that ran behind the building.

Halting there in the darkness, he waited until his eyes were fully adjusted to the change in light and, certain that no one was close by, hurried to O'Hara's where he stood by silently while the hostler saddled and bridled the roan.

10

"You be coming back?" the overalled man asked as he led the gelding into the runway.

"I'll be back," Sutton answered, swinging to the saddle. *Anyway, I'm hoping to,* he added silently as he walked the horse out into the open.

He rode northward for the Bovey place, keeping out of sight as much as possible, carefully circling the ranch houses and other homesteaders that were *en route.* Now and then something within the man checked him and he would hesitate and listen for any sounds of pursuit — and once he circled wide, cut back for a good half mile before he was completely satisfied that there was no one on his trail.

Such precaution was second nature with Ben Sutton. He took a few minutes, always aware that in his line of work one small mistake could be his last, and now, as he drifted quietly and steadily along through the night, seeing the friendly lights of different homes along the way, it came to him that, actually, it was a hell of a way to live — and what a fine thing it would be to have a place of his own and a wife waiting for him at sundown. A wife such as Martha Murdock . . .

He shifted on the saddle, a little surprised and somewhat disturbed that she should find a place in his thoughts. But she was there and he found himself remembering how she looked and the sound of her voice and the way sunlight had danced upon her hair when she stepped out into the open. The thought was not good; likely when Martha learned his identity and purpose, she would only think the worst of him.

11

It would be a fine thing to settle down, and of late the idea had been coming into his mind more and more. Could he do it? Could he really live like other men? That question, too, had entered his consideration. What would it be like not to be forever on the move, not following out some outlaw's trail, not climbing an endless hill or riding fast across a wide, flat mesa in a desperate effort to ward off trouble?

What would it feel like to walk down the street of a town without viewing every passerby with suspicion? How would it seem never again to have trouble bending overhead like a dark, threatening cloud, or feel the weight of a gun on your hip and the pressure of a cartridge belt around your belly? Would he ever know?

Deep within him were strong doubts. He had no illusions about himself, his job, or the ruthless nature of the man with whom he was compelled to deal. Somewhere along the line there was always and inevitably a man who got lucky or who was able to draw his pistol and get off a shot just a trace faster. Such was as certain as darkness followed daylight — and the smart ones bore that in mind and got out in time.

He'd do that, too. He meant to all along. So far, however, the time just hadn't shaped up to where it was possible. Mainly — the law wasn't ready. He wouldn't turn in his special officer badge yet — not until he was certain in his own mind that the regularly constituted lawmen could handle any and all problems that arose.

He topped out a grassy roll, looked down upon the Bovey place. It lay in a wide field that backed against a

12

small creek, flowing like a strip of polished silver through the moonlight. It was a small homestead, of the type that cattlemen hated but that would someday sprinkle the country, and Sutton, viewing the ramshackle buildings moodily, thought: *Even he's got more than I've got.*

As he watched, the yellow square of light in a window blanked out. Bovey had retired. Urging the roan forward at a slow walk, he descended the slope and pulled to a stop next to a slab shed, pleased that no dogs had heard or seen him and set up their racket.

He sat quietly in the saddle, a lonely man doing a lonely thing, and let his mind stray. Around him in the night were all the pleasant, earthy smells of a farm, the muted, satisfying noises of livestock in the barn. Far off in the hills to the east a coyote barked, and once there was the swish of broad, set wings as a hunting owl passed swiftly by. Unexpectedly the roan blew, stamped. Sutton came up sharply, tense, afraid someone inside the house had heard and appeared, but the place remained dark, and he settled back, relieved.

And then, from the south, came the drumming tattoo of fast-running horses. At once all else faded from Ben Sutton's mind, and, slipping from the roan, he drew up close to the shed near which he waited, listening intently. At least a half dozen riders, he guessed, possibly more. Shortly the drumming ceased as if a halt had been called, but he realized they had simply pulled down to a walk in order to deaden the noise of their coming.

When at last they came into sight, he saw there were ten men in all, each wearing a head mask of white cloth that hung to their shoulders and lending them a ghostly, square face with round, empty eyes. They ranged up before the Bovey place in a shallow half circle, and the leader, advancing a few steps, drew his gun. The sound exploded into the night, set off a chain of echoes.

Almost at once a light blossomed inside the structure, and Sutton, moving silently, eased forward in the shadows until he stood at the corner of the house. In the next moment the door creaked and the homesteader, a ludicrous figure in a long, white nightshirt, lamp held overhead, came out into the yard. He stared at the line of riders and then, voice pitched in alarm, cried: "Vigilantes!"

"Bovey," the leader said, "appears we've made a mistake."

"Mistake? How . . . what's that mean?"

"We shouldn't've let you and your kind ever squat in this country. For cattle . . . not sodbustin' . . ."

"But we're down here in the valley. Ain't no cattle raising done along here. We ain't bothering you none."

"You're helping yourself to our beef sure is," another of the masked men cut in harshly. "Got to stop."

"I ain't never touched any of your stock . . . before God, I swear it!"

"We know better, Bovey. Now, get your woman and young 'uns out of that shack . . . we're burning it down."

Sutton, anger rising swiftly within him, moved forward. Hand resting on the butt of the gun, he threw his flat voice into the sudden hush.

"This stops right here!"

Bovey wheeled, startled by his appearance. The vigilante leader struggled with his horse briefly while behind him a mutter of words broke out. At once the night became tense.

"Who the hell are you, mister?"

Ben Sutton moved farther into the open. In the pale light his face was a cold, expressionless mask. "Makes no difference who I am . . . point is, you're not the law. If you've got any complaints against this man, take them to the marshal or the nearest sheriff."

One of the masked men laughed. "Can see he's a stranger . . . telling us to go to Gilcrist!"

The vigilante leader nodded. "That's right . . . we're the only law around here . . . we've got to be. Marshal don't amount to a hill of beans."

"Still represents the law . . . and it's up to you to respect it. Something you . . . all of you . . . better get straight. This is a territory of the United States. It's under civil government, and there's no room in it for masked riders running around taking matters into their own hands."

"Government . . . hell! What good's that? Where was the god-damned government when we needed some help? Where was it when that wild bunch from Colorado rode in here and raided our herds? Where was it when the Jenson gang come sashaying through here, shooting up everything . . . and killing my pa and ma?

15

I'll tell you where, Mister Buttinsky . . . setting on their tails in Santa Fé, doing nothing!"

A sigh passed through Ben Sutton. The minds of men worked in direct, bitter ways; always they justified their acts of vengeance by misguided thoughts of personally meted out justice which had its birth in some terrible experience that warped and soured them beyond reason. He could understand their desire, but he could not condone it. Such was the purpose of the law.

And he knew now for sure who the leader of the vigilantes — the Justice Committee as they called themselves — actually was: Yancey Murdock. It had been his parents the Jenson bunch had senselessly murdered.

"And what about the Gilpins? They sure didn't get no help when . . ."

"All right, all right," Sutton broke in. "That's all in the past. This is right now, and things've changed. Like I said, if you have something to charge this man with, go to the marshal, tell him."

"And if we don't want to do it that way?"

"Then you've got trouble on your hands. I'm an officer of the law, special . . . out of the governor's office. You try going ahead and you've got me to crawl over."

"Won't be no chore," one of the men said. "Odds are plenty our way."

"Maybe . . . but there'll be six of you who won't see the sun come up. I'll get that many of you before I'm finished."

Murdock was leaning forward on his saddle. "Somebody send for you?" he asked in a suspicious voice. "One of these squatters, maybe?"

"No," Ben said flatly, and dropped it there. "Now, what's it to be? We handling this the way it's supposed to be, a trial for this man before a judge and jury . . . or is to be bloodshed? Choice is yours. You figure you . . ."

Ben Sutton's words broke off as a warning shot through him. His ears picked up the faintest of sounds. Instinctively he dodged to one side, started to wheel. In the next fragment of time something solid crashed into his head and he went spinning down into a black void.

He seemed to be fighting his way upward, out of a deep pit. He felt a cool cloth touch his forehead, and, as the veil of cobwebs tore, began to fade from his mind, he heard Bovey's voice.

"Just you rest easy, mister . . . you're going to be all right."

He stirred impatiently, tried to rise. Pain, in a shocking wave, struck him. He sank back once again, descended into the darkness.

He opened his eyes much later. It was near dawn, and he could hear a rooster crowing proudly nearby. He was inside the homesteader's, lying on a corn-shuck mattress placed on a crudely made bed. Bovey and a worn-looking woman with stringy hair were looking down at him. He sat up slowly as if testing each inch. There was little pain although his head ached. Pivoting, he threw his legs over the edge of the bed.

17

"Stay right there," the homesteader said then. "The wife'll get you a cup of coffee . . . what you're needing."

Sutton murmured his assent. A stiff shot of whiskey would be more to the heart of things, but he made no mention of it and accepted the thick crockery cup of steaming liquid, downed it.

"Obliged to you," he said, nodding to the woman, and then turned his eyes to Bovey. "You see who hit me?"

The homesteader shook his head. "Never seen hardly anything. There you was standing there, next thing I knowed you was falling . . ."

Sutton swore silently. He had failed. Oh, sure, he had prevented the night riders from burning down the Bovey place, but that was secondary to his way of thinking. Where he had failed was in proving the strength and invincibility of organized law.

"You think it was one of those masked men?" he asked, rising. He made the move too quickly, was forced to stand motionless, eyes clasped shut, while a wave of nausea rolled through him.

"No, sir, don't figure it was. Can't figure it out why, but I think it was somebody else altogether. And them vigilantes, they was about as surprised as me."

The unsteadiness passed. Ben opened his eyes, found Mrs. Bovey standing beside him, another cup of coffee in her hand. Her colorless lips parted into a smile of sorts.

"I'd be right pleased to fix you something to eat. Got some bacon and eggs . . . or maybe you'd want . . ."

"Coffee's doing the job fine," Sutton said, and again thanked her.

His mind was clearing rapidly now, functioning as it should despite the dull aching. He had his own doubts, too, where his attacker was concerned. He would have noticed one of the riders moving away, circling to get in behind him, and the entire group had pulled up in front of Bovey's, with no thought given to encircling the place. No, it was someone else, an outsider. Who? It occurred to him then that the only other person who would know that he intended to be at Bovey's that night was Amos Whitcomb.

At that realization all conjecture and speculation came to a halt on dead center. Whitcomb! It didn't make sense — yet, perhaps it did. But it actually didn't matter for the moment, anyway. It was a side issue, one to be fathomed out later. The important thing was that he knew the leader of the masked men — the Justice Committee — who were riding the hills, terrorizing all with their kind of law, and that was the key to the situation he had been directed to correct.

"Where's the Murdock Ranch from here?" he asked, moving toward the door.

"About ten mile west," Bovey answered. He bent forward, peered closely at Ben. "You sure you're up to riding, mister? Maybe you ought to wait . . ."

"I'm fine . . . that my hat over there on the table?"

The homesteader reached for Sutton's headgear, passed it to him. A frown clouded his face. "About all that fuss last night . . . ain't you even going to ask if I done what they claimed . . . stole that beef?"

19

"Not my business to ask," Sutton replied, "only to see that you get a fair hearing in a court if somebody wants to charge you with it. I'm interested in the law being used right . . . nothing else."

The homesteader bobbed his head. "Well, I'm mighty thankful you was here. My old woman and me and the kids'd sure be out in the cold right now if you hadn't . . . and maybe it'd've been worse. They've done strung up a couple or so they claimed was rustling . . . caught them at it, was told. And then they burned down the Ellermyers' and the Simpsons', drove them clean out of the country."

"A body just ain't safe!" Mrs. Bovey wailed suddenly from the kitchen. "I ain't staying around here no longer . . . and that's the gospel."

"It'll be safe from here on," the homesteader said. "We're going to have a good law now. Folks'll be able to go about their business and not be scared."

"Ain't going to make no difference! Between them there cattlemen and gangs like them Jensons, decent folks can't . . ."

Sutton stepped out into the yard, waited on the sagging stoop while one of Bovey's older children led the roan to him, smiled shyly, and hurried away. Shoving his toe into the stirrup, Ben swung onto the saddle. The homesteader moved up beside him, his face sober.

"Mister, I'm mighty grateful for what you done, and I'm saying it again. Now, is there something that you're wanting me to do to sort of straighten things out with this law you're fixing to put in here?"

"Not putting it in . . . it's already here and has been since General Kearney came through nearly thirty years ago. People in this part of the territory have just ignored it. You want to do right by it, go into town and talk to the marshal. Tell him you've been accused of cattle rustling and you want either to be tried before a judge for it . . . or you want the people accusing you of it to shut up and make you an apology."

Bovey stared. "Them cattle growers . . . apologize to me?"

"What they'll have to do . . . unless they're right."

The homesteader drew himself up stiffly. "Well, they sure ain't right! I never stoled nothing in my life." He bobbed his head decisively. "All right, mister, I'll do it. I'm going in and talk to the marshal today."

"The right thing to do," Ben Sutton said, smiling, and rode out of the yard.

He traveled leisurely in the warm morning sunshine, pointing due west, letting the roan choose his way while he mulled the events of the last hours over in his mind. Few things were making sense, other than the fact that he knew definitely the identity of the Justice Committee's leader, and that was, after all, most important. But who, if not one of their members, would wish to stop him? That it could be Amos Whitcomb didn't seem logical; neither did it seem likely that it was one of the men who had attempted to ambush him. They would not have wasted their time on simply knocking him unconscious — their intent was to kill.

The solution to that lay in the future — after he had settled with Yancey Murdock, which was now at hand he saw, as the road turned sharply into a wide, cottonwood-shaded yard in which stood a cluster of well-tended, neatly painted buildings that immediately brought to him the thought: *This is the kind of place I'd like to have.*

Walking the gelding up to the hitch rack where two horses stood, hip-slacked, he stepped down. The sweet smell of honeysuckle hung in the clean air, and he had hesitated, motionless, caught up by that when the screen door of the house opened and Martha Murdock came out onto the porch to greet him.

"Why, it's Mister Sutton!" she said, pleased. "It's nice of you to drop by."

He nodded, fumbled off his hat while a strange, disturbing sensation coursed through him, turning him awkward, thickening his tongue. He murmured something in reply, checked himself, grateful for the appearance of Yancey Murdock in that exact moment. The young rancher emerged from the office he maintained at the lower end of the gallery, eyed Ben coldly.

"What's on your mind?" he asked in a hostile voice.

Martha turned to her brother in surprise. "Oh, you know each other!"

"Some," Yancey said, and waited for Sutton to answer.

Ben shrugged. He preferred to discuss matters in private, particularly not in front of Martha, but Murdock seemed not to care.

22

"I'm here about last night," he said. "You think having one of your bunch hit me over the head would make any difference?"

"Had nothing to do with that," the rancher said sharply. "Don't know who it was . . . and he was gone before we could find out."

Sutton had guessed that was the way of it, but he wanted to be certain. He glanced at the girl, almost regretfully said: "I'm serving notice on you, Murdock . . . officially . . . you're to disband this vigilante committee you're leading. Time for that kind of thing is over . . . finished."

From the tail of his eye Ben saw Martha stiffen, move to her brother's side. Evidently she knew of the masked men.

Yancy shook his head. "All right, you've given me the notice. Means nothing. We'll still have to look after things up here."

"No . . . it's done with. Maybe there was a time when it was necessary, but no longer. The law will take care of any such problems."

"Law!" Murdock echoed scornfully. "What law? That old man down in town that's wearing a badge? That what you mean by the law?"

"He represents the law," Sutton said quietly, "and maybe, if you and your masked avengers had gotten with him and backed him up when things started going wrong . . . he'd be the law. But you took it on yourselves, instead. All right, if that's what the problem is, I'll see that you get a new marshal . . . a tough one who'll handle things to suit even you!"

Yancey Murdock frowned. "We don't want no gun-slinger running around here loose."

"What do you think you and your committee are? You're even worse . . . jumping at rumors, punishing a man when you don't know anything for sure . . . hanging, murdering just because you think you're right. A hired gun, at least, usually knows for sure why he kills."

Martha's hand was on her brother's arm. "Yancey . . . maybe he's right. Maybe you should let the law . . ."

The sharp, flat crack of a rifle sliced through her words. In that same fraction of an instant Ben Sutton felt a bullet tug at his sleeve, whirled. Three men on horses were silhouetted on a ridge only yards away. The last of the Denison gang — he recognized one of them this time. He'd been right. They had dogged his trail ever since Magdalena, had made their try in Navajo Cañon, failed, and were here now to settle it once and for all — claim their vengeance or die in the attempt.

"Get Martha inside!" he yelled at Murdock and, drawing his pistol, started zigzagging up the slope that led to where the riders had halted.

"I'll get my gun . . . give you a hand!" Yancey shouted, grasping the girl's arm, rushing her toward the house.

"No . . . this is my problem . . . the law's!" Sutton yelled back without slowing. "I'll take care of it!"

He heard Yancey make some sort of reply as he pressed on, but he did not catch the words. The Denisons were firing steadily at him but his erratic course and their own nervous horses were making accuracy impossible. He plunged on, holding back his return fire until he was in better range, feeling the muscles of his legs beginning to tighten under the strain of running uphill, his breathing to grow more difficult.

A bullet ripped across his arm, tearing through the sleeve of his shirt, slicing a groove in the skin. He paused then, aimed at the man nearest him, squeezed off a shot. The rider threw up his arms, fell sideways from his saddle. Cool, ignoring another bullet plucking at his leg, Ben Sutton leveled his weapon at the man in the center, triggered his weapon. The outlaw buckled forward, tumbled to the sandy ground. Sutton threw himself to one side then, wanting to offer no better target. Motion to his far left sent a warning through him — two riders coming along the road. He swore softly, threw himself full length, pistol leveled at the last man on the ridge.

Surprise and relief rolled through him. The rider had dropped his weapon to the ground, had raised his hands above his head in a sign of surrender. Immediately Sutton transferred his attention to the approaching men — and again heaved a sigh. It was Bovey, the homesteader, and with him was Marshal Lon Gilcrist.

Ben got to his feet, motioned to the man on the ridge who rode forward slowly, started down the slope. When he drew abreast, Sutton said — "Get off . . . walk." — and, when the man complied, followed him down into Murdock's yard where Bovey and Gilcrist were joining Martha and Yancey.

25

"Your prisoner," Sutton said to the old lawman, shoving the outlaw toward him. "I'll be in, make out the charges."

Gilcrist dug a pair of chain-linked cuffs from his saddle-bags, put them about the man's wrists, then handed the key to Ben. "Maybe you won't be wanting me to, after you hear what I've got to say."

Sutton looked at the marshal more closely. On beyond him, he could see Martha smiling at him proudly, hear Yancey telling Bovey and several of the ranch hands who had been attracted by the gunshots of the incident. "Damndest thing I ever saw. Them three lined up there on that ridge, shooting at him . . . and him charging them like he was the whole U.S. Cavalry! If that's the kind of law . . ."

"I'm listening," Sutton said to the lawman.

Gilcrist squared his thin shoulders. "Was me that hit you over the head last night."

Sutton drew up in surprise. Yancey Murdock and the others fell silent, equally startled.

"You . . . why?" Ben demanded in a tight voice.

"Knew what you'd come to Mexican Springs for. Got it from a deputy in Santa Fé . . . said the governor was sending you to straighten things out . . . figured I knew, I reckon, me being the marshal."

"Why didn't you speak up when we were talking? I'd have brought you in on it if I thought you knew."

"Didn't know just what I ought to be doing. Anyway, I followed you out to Bovey's, and, when it looked like you was about to take over, force the committee to quit, I stepped in."

"Why? . . . I'll ask it again," Sutton pressed.

"Good reason . . . knowed that I couldn't handle things alone, but long as the Justice Committee kept riding the hills, outlaw gangs like the Jensons and rustlers and such would stay clear of us . . . was the only way I could see to keep law and order. Your just coming up here once, then pulling out, leaving us, won't help none."

A surge of anger rolled through Ben Sutton. This was the sort of thing he had to fight — this selfishness, this single-minded kind of personal law — this type of self-preservation! And then he felt a wave of pity.

He was wrong to condemn lawmen such as Lon Gilcrist. In number they were pitifully few when compared to the outlaws they were forced to contend with — and all worked under great odds, quite often bucked strong opposition from the very people they sought to protect. He should not blame Lon Gilcrist for taking advantage of any and every opportunity for holding the lawless element at bay.

"Well, I don't think we'll be needing the Justice Committee any longer," Yancey Murdock said, stepping up beside the old lawman and laying an arm across his shoulder. "And I don't figure you need to worry none about keeping things peaceful . . . not if that's the kind of law Sutton's talking about."

Ben nodded. "It is . . . the kind that handles the outlaws without folks taking things into their own hands."

Gilcrist shook his head. "Just . . . just don't see how I can . . . alone."

"You're not alone. Every town in the territory's got or will have a good, honest lawman."

"But I'm getting old and . . ."

"Makes no difference. Point is the people will stand behind you . . . and that's what makes the law . . . people backing up the man they elected to wear a star. With that happening all over the country, the day of the outlaw will soon pass."

"Amen to that," Bovey murmured.

Yancey Murdock nodded briskly to Gilcrist. "I can see what he means, Marshal . . . and you'll get your backing up from here on. I'll see to it." He paused, turned to Sutton. "Big county, howsomever, and we don't have a sheriff right now. Job's open to you if you want it . . . know other ranchers and homesteaders would be for it. Or maybe you'd like to get a place of your own . . . raise cattle . . ."

Ben stared off across the smooth hills, remembering all the things he'd like to do, to have, remembering, too, the endless days, the lonely nights, fully aware in those moments of Martha, standing at the edge of the porch, her eyes bright with promise, lips parted in a hopeful smile — a life with her, a ranch of his own. Peace, the end of danger, of trouble, of loneliness.

And then he had a quick realization of that worn, harried man in the Governor's Palace in Santa Fé, with all his great plans for the territory, and he thought of all the other Lon Gilcrists needing help, struggling to make the badge they wore mean something — and he knew that it could never be. The law was a part of him — a second heart, perhaps — and he would be duty-bound and forever obligated to serve it until one day it could stand alone, unassisted, and not be challenged.

He did not look at Martha, simply nodded to Yancey, said: "Obliged for the offer, but I reckon I'd better keep working at what I'm doing." Moving to his horse, he went to the saddle, settled himself, threw his attention to Gilcrist.

"Marshal, expect we'd better get the prisoner to your jail. Then I'd best be on my way."

Gilcrist motioned the last of the Denisons to his mount, climbed onto his own horse. Yancey Murdock stepped forward, extended his hand to Ben.

"Like you to know there'll always be a place at our table for you."

Sutton smiled. "Appreciate that . . . and maybe someday I'll just drop by." Only then did he raise his eyes to meet those of Martha. "*Adiós*," he said softly, and, wheeling the roan about, rode out of the yard.

The Homecoming

Matt Sowers pulled his bay horse to a halt at the edge of Willow's single street and considered the settlement. Dusty, bone-tired, he sat loosely in the saddle as he studied the town. It had changed little, he saw. The same desolate, sun-scoured look, the same yellow dust haze that had hung in the hot, motionless air that day when Harley Percale, of the mighty Rocking Star Ranch, had succeeded in goading him to the limit — and died for his efforts.

Matt still remembered the way the echoes of the gunshots had bounced back and forth between the sagging, shabby buildings, the smell of burned powder, and the shocked faces of those who had witnessed the incident — shocked, horrified, and filled with fear when they realized it was a Percale who had been killed. Sowers had been young then, a raw kid actually, and later, when the meaning of what he'd done had sunk in and he'd had a glimpse of the Percale outfit taking the town apart as they searched for him, he'd climbed onto his horse and ridden out.

Something within Sowers stirred, softening momentarily the hard corners of his angular face as his eyes drifted over the familiar, weather-worn structures. Along the endless trails he had followed in those years after he had run, he'd never found a settlement that dislodged Willow from his mind despite the hostility he knew it had for him, and strangers met along the way had forever remained strangers — it just was not in his make-up to unbend, lay aside the cool indifference that had become a part of him, and become openly friendly.

He wondered now if those who lived in the town had changed any, if the passage of years had dulled their resentment toward him for the trouble he had brought down upon their heads. Matt had a moment's hope that such could be, but it was quickly forgotten; being a realist, he knew that he was out of thought and mind only as long as he was out of sight.

Just as the Percales would remember, so would they. The old wound would reopen, and it would be just as it had been five years or so ago. But for him it could not be otherwise. All time for consideration was behind him — left along the trails near Silver City, and Tucson, and Nogales, and half a hundred other places where he had fought it out in his mind under a hot sun, or during the still, breathless nights. It was his right to return, to face down trouble, and reclaim his own life — and nothing save death was going to change that decision. Shrugging, he raked the bay lightly with his spurs, sent him moving forward.

Stiff-backed, he rode dead center down the street, seeing but not acknowledging any of the startled looks flung his way as he traveled the full distance to Whitman's Stable. Reining in there, he swung down, and handed the leathers to the hostler who appeared from the depths of the building's shadowy, redolent interior.

"Tend him," Matt said. "I'll be wanting him again about dark."

Coming about, Sowers crossed the dusty street and entered the hotel, pausing briefly inside the doorway while his eyes took in the small lobby. Finding it deserted, he stepped up to the desk where a clerk idly thumbed through a yellowing magazine.

"How about a room?"

The man looked up. His jaw sagged. "Sowers?" he said in a strangled voice.

"Right," Matt replied coolly. "What about a room?"

The clerk, a middle-aged man in nondescript clothing, pushed his steel-rimmed glasses back on his nose. "Well ... I ain't so sure. Don't want no trouble ..."

"Won't be any," Sowers said in a patient voice. "I figure to move back into my own place tomorrow after I clean it up some."

The clerk stared. "You aiming to stay?"

"I am. How about a room?"

The man's thin shoulders stirred. Opening a dog-eared register, he shoved it and a pencil stub across the counter to Matt, who scrawled his name on the specified line.

"Take Number Five," the clerk said when that was done. "Key's in the door. Can pay me now. Two dollars."

Sowers laid the silver dollars on the desk, and turned away. The man's voice checked him.

"What about the Percales? Shub and Austin are still around . . . and they won't be forgetting."

Matt came back around slowly. "So?" he murmured.

The clerk frowned, picked up the coins. "Well . . . I was just a-wondering," he said hesitantly.

"Don't," Sowers said in the same cool voice. "My problem . . . not yours," and made his way to his room.

Entering, he closed the door and turned the key in the lock. A hard-cornered smile pulled at his mouth as he stood, motionless, in the warm gloom. The clerk, by that moment, was probably already busy spreading the news of his return, and any who had not seen him ride in would now be aware of his presence. Considering that wryly, he moved then to the iron bedstead, and with a deep sigh stretched out full length upon it, enjoying immediately the simple pleasure of complete rest.

It was, he noted, glancing about, a room just like all the other hotel rooms he had seen: dry, peeling wallpaper, scarred furniture, dust-streaked windows, and the inevitable chipped china pitcher and bowl. A worn carpet covered the floor, and a single picture — cut no doubt from a calendar furnished by some Eastern concern — graced a wall. He studied the faded likeness on the thick paper — that of a young woman sitting, prim and proud, in a shiny, red-wheeled buggy drawn by a fine-looking black horse.

Immediately his thoughts turned to Laurie Collister and the memory of her, that he so often had driven from his mind, had its strong and moving way with him again. Was she still there in Willow? Had she married?

He remembered her as he had last seen her, standing near the gate of the Collister place when he rode by, hand raised in farewell, her words — "I'll be here when you come back." — barely audible to him.

But that had been a long time ago — and he had never written or sent any word to her. No doubt she was now only a part of his past. Turned restless as always by such thoughts, Sowers drew himself to a sitting position. For a long minute he stared moodily at the scarred and dusty toes of his boots, and then finally, unable to remain inactive further, rose, washed, and, returning to the street, took up a stand just outside the hotel's doorway.

The afternoon's heat still laid its restriction on the town, and he was not surprised at its deserted appearance. Such could be deceiving, however, and caution, ever a factor in his life now, held him, motionless, while his eyes probed thoroughly along the quiet buildings and into the passageways lying between them. Satisfied that he had nothing to fear at the moment, and suddenly feeling the need for food, Matt crossed over to the town's only restaurant, and entered. Selecting a back table that gave him command of the door, he sat down, and ordered his meal. He ate casually, relishing the steak, beans, hot biscuits, and coffee, and, when he was finished, paid the check to the restaurant's owner — a stranger who regarded him narrowly — and moved once more to the outside.

The word would be out by that time for certain, and he should be seeing some reaction to his return, he knew, as his eyes again laid their sharp search along the street. Oddly there was no sign of anyone. A spark of hope sprang to life in Matt's breast. Perhaps time had healed the wound! Maybe the Percales, and Willow, had forgotten! Sowers had a moment of pleasure in the speculation of the possibility, and then wiped it from his mind as the swinging doors of Kelly's Saloon flung open, and half a dozen men spilled out into the street and headed purposefully toward him.

Taut, but outwardly at ease, Matt continued to roll the cigarette he had started, and watched the men approach. Shub Percale and his twin brother Austin were slightly in advance of the others — all Rocking Star cowhands probably — and, as they came to a halt before him, they drew up shoulder to shoulder while the cowhands fanned out to either side. The Percales looked much the same, Sowers noted, a bit thinner and older perhaps, but otherwise there was little change.

"What the hell you doing back?" Shub demanded, hooking his thumbs in his gun belt.

Matt, the cigarette finished, hung it between his lips, coolly struck a match with a thumbnail, lit the thin cylinder of paper and tobacco, and, drawing in, exhaled a small cloud of smoke. Flipping the match into the dust, he nodded.

"Happens I live here," he said quietly.

"The hell you do!" Shub yelled. "You been run out, and, by God, you best stay out or . . ."

"Or what?" Sowers pressed when Percale hesitated. Then: "Better get this straight, Shub . . . all of you, in fact . . . I'm here to stay. I won't run again. Things've changed."

"Like what?"

"I ain't no kid now."

Sowers had known this moment would come. He had realized it five years ago when he was less than a mile from Willow and it came to him that he had let the Percales drive him from his home. He should not have permitted them to do it, he had told himself over and over during the long, empty years that followed; he should have stood his ground — but he had been young then, too young to know what a man should do.

"Can't see as that'll make a difference," Austin said.

"Something you can sure find out in a hurry," Matt replied with a half smile. "I killed one of you Percales, and I sure don't want to kill any more of you. I'm only looking for peace and a chance to start living my life again here in my home town, but if . . ."

"Keep your hands away from them guns!"

Sowers saw the tension break in the men confronting him, and heard the slam of a screen door as the tall figure of a man wearing a town marshal's star appeared suddenly, and moved in between him and the Percales. A new lawman. Evidently old Abe Quinley had moved on — or died.

"Appears to me you Percales are wanting to start trouble," he said, folding his arms and facing the men.

Shub shook his head angrily. "Keep out of this, Tinsley . . . this is something that happened before your time."

"Man there's Matt Sowers," Austin added. "He killed our brother Harley."

"Was a fair fight, I've been told," the lawman said. "And far as it happening before my time, that don't mean nothing. I'm interested in what happens in my town now."

"Meaning?" Austin's voice had a wary quality to it.

"Meaning I won't stand for no shootings . . . no matter what the reason. If you . . ."

"Better look at your hole card, old man," Shub cut in. "You're going up against the Rocking Star if you . . ."

Tinsley laughed. "Don't try impressing me, mister! You seem to think that you Percales set at the right hand of God. Well, I don't . . . and, if I did, it wouldn't matter one whit to me. I'm the law here, and I aim to keep the peace. This man's got a right to be here, and I figure to see that nobody tries taking it away from him."

"In plain words . . . you're siding with a killer."

"Not how I heard it . . . and, if you're talking about his gunning down somebody else, somewhere else, that's a horse of a different color . . . and will need proving."

"Proof?" Austin echoed. "Hell, there's been plenty of talk about him."

"Talk ain't nothing . . . and a bad reputation starts mighty easy," the lawman broke in. "And it can build fast . . . so fast that a man can be hard put deciding whether he ought to try and live up to it, or try and live it down. Now, I ain't saying one way or another about this man, but I do know there ain't no wanted dodgers out for him, and that's good enough for me."

Percale shook his head, frowned. "You're picking the wrong side in this, Marshal," he said, and turned his attention to Sowers, silent through the exchange. "Be gone by sunrise, or it'll be like it was five years ago," he told Matt, and, wheeling, led the others back into Kelly's.

Tinsley watched until the swinging doors had stilled, then faced Matt. A lean, graying man, he had a thin, straight mouth, and small, hard eyes.

"Want you to get this straight, Sowers . . . I ain't taking nobody's side in this but the law's."

Matt nodded. "Good enough for me," he said, and, recrossing the street, entered the hotel.

Near dark found him astride his horse and traveling along the rutty road toward the Collister place. There had been no one in town he could ask about Laurie, and now as the moment approached when he would — or would not — see her, a vague uneasiness filled him, and he pulled in the bay uncertain for the moment as to his own desires. Seeing her, finding out that she belonged to another man would be hard to take; still, he had to know.

But he delayed, letting his eyes drift, follow the low, rolling land softening now in the fading light. He could see the narrow, winding strip of green that marked the course of the river, and beyond that the short hills, browned over at this time of year by the summer sun. To the right five miles would be the Percales' Rocking Star Ranch, while farther on, and to his left, would be his small spread — or what now remained of it — passed on to him when his parents died.

He pictured it as it had been, lying in a shallow valley, the cottonwoods arching over the house that he, as a boy, had helped his father build. The flowers his mother planted yearly would, of course, be gone, and the well likely was dry, but the land, changeless and everlasting, would still be there — waiting. It was his — his place, his home, and he would reclaim it in spite of the Percales, and the town of Willow, if that was the way the cards fell. But it would be nice if Laurie Collister was to share it with him.

He rode on, minutes later topped a rise, and looked down upon the cluster of buildings that was the Collister place. A yellow square of lamplight in a window drew him on, and, coming in close, he circled the house and drew up at the hitch rack in the rear. Dismounting, he walked the short distance to where he could look through the open door, into the kitchen. Laurie was sitting at the table alone, reading. For a full minute he watched her, drinking in the soft beauty of her features, the wealth of hair that capped her head, the quiet intent of her manner, and then he could wait no longer; he must know where he stood.

"Laurie," he called softly, and stepped into the room.

The girl's head came up quickly, and her eyes filled with disbelief. Her lips parted in surprise, and then suddenly she was on her feet and rushing into his arms.

"Oh, Matt . . . I've hoped . . . prayed! It's been so long!"

"Five years," he murmured, holding her close. "I was scared you'd not be here . . . that I'd lost you."

"I was afraid, too, afraid you'd never come back."

"Oughtn't to have gone in the first place. Was a mistake. But I'm back now . . . back to stay. Nothing . . . nobody will drive me away . . . unless they kill me."

They stood there silently then, lost in the magic of the moment, each dwelling in their own depth of happiness. At last she spoke, voicing a worry that came suddenly to her.

"You've been in town?"

He nodded. "Seems nothing's changed."

"Then there's trouble . . . ?"

Sowers's wide shoulders lifted, fell. "Nothing I didn't expect . . . and can't handle," he said, and dismissed the subject. "Now, I want to tell you something good. Like I've said, I'm back to stay, and, if things are the same between us, we can get married and move into my place, start a spread of our own. I've got the money to do all the things that'll need doing, and . . ."

He broke off, feeling a stillness come over her, and he looked down into the oval of her face, wondering at the cause. Laurie pulled back slightly.

"The money," she began haltingly. "Did you . . . ?"

Anger and impatience rose within him. "Did I make it working at a job, or did I get it with a gun . . . that what you're trying to ask?"

The girl bit at her lips. "There's been talk . . . rumors that you hire out . . . that you take pay to kill men . . ."

Matt's arms dropped to his sides, and a cool aloofness was abruptly upon him. He stepped back, and for several minutes stared off into the closing darkness beyond the door.

"Does it make a difference?"

Laurie didn't answer, and they stood there each utterly alone although mere inches apart. It was in his power to end the tension for he could have told her of the many months spent riding guard for a bullion train in Arizona, or the endless days he had served as outrider for a freight line plying danger-filled Indian country, of the countless jobs he had worked at to accumulate his stake, but his stubborn pride forbade it, sealing his lips and turning him inward.

"Then . . . then it's true? You are a . . . a paid killer, and you won't hesitate to kill any . . . ?"

"I'll fight for what's mine," Sowers replied stiffly, and, pivoting, walked out into the coming night.

It was like Matt Sowers to reconcile himself to an inevitable fact; he had lost Laurie Collister, and he had no choice but to face up to it. The likelihood that such would be the way of it had been in his mind throughout the long years during which he was wandering across the frontier, and he had more or less conditioned himself to the possibility.

Thus the loss did not strike him with as much force as it might have — not that he still did not hunger for her, and want a life with her. Laurie would always be a part of him, regardless, and realizing that it was not to be was like closing a door somewhere within his being. But there was no other answer; Laurie was uncertain — actually had doubts about him, and Matt Sowers was wise enough to know that doubt, like a festering wound, grew worse with time.

Riding slowly he came to the fork where the road cut away to the east, and, pulling the bay to a stop, he sat for a time, gazing moodily out across the hills and flats. Moonlight flooded the warm night, laying a pale glow upon everything, and thousands of stars winked down from a bed of black velvet while the soft hush that claimed the land was almost tangible. Well off in the distance a coyote flung his discordant challenge into the stillness, and immediately from the direction of the Percale Ranch a dog answered with a round of frantic barking.

Still moved by a desire to see his place Matt urged the bay on, shortly turning left to follow a vaguely familiar road that led him deeper into the low, round-topped hills. An hour or so later he broke over the last rise, and looked down upon the ranch. A flood of memories welled through him, and, spurring his horse, he anxiously hurried on. Reaching the gate, sagging from a single leather hinge, he dismounted, entered the weedy yard, and covered the remaining distance on foot, each step reawakening old scenes and memories of long-forgotten incidents.

As near as he could tell, the house wasn't in too bad a condition, and the barn in which his father had taken such pride appeared strong and solid. The corrals, the sheds, and other structures, however, were in various stages of disrepair, and the fenced-in area built to confine his mother's chickens but from which they continually had escaped was now only a single, upright corner post and a snarl of rusting wire.

It wouldn't take much to put the ranch in shape, Matt thought. He could make it livable for himself, use most of his cash to buy cattle, and then, when . . .

Sowers drew up suddenly, hearing the steady drum of horses coming in from the south and, instinctively cautious, stepped into the shadows alongside the house. Two riders, at an easy lope, silhouetted briefly on the hill beyond the barn, and then disappeared. Matt listened as grass-muffled hoof beats swung past the cluster of buildings, and then died. Instantly on the alert and suspicious, he moved from the darkness and threw a searching glance toward the barn. Vague, indefinite motion caught his eyes. A moment later a match flared in the blackness within the structure, and the outline of a man bending over a pile of straw and trash became distinct.

"No!" Matt yelled, and started across the yard at a hard run.

The match went out, and a tiny flame leaped up from the straw. A gun suddenly laced the night with its orange tongue. Sowers felt the breath of the bullet as it sped past him. Diving headlong to the ground, he brought up his own gun, but the two trespassers were already lost in the shadows, and gained their horses and were rushing off into the night.

Cursing, Matt scrambled to his feet and ran the distance to the barn where he trampled the mounting fire to ashes.

Hard set, anger boiling through him, Sowers stood silently as he realized what would have happened had he not been present. The men — two of the Rocking Star cowhands he'd seen with the Percales earlier, he was certain — would not have stopped at firing the barn, but would have put a flaming torch to the house as well, all undoubtedly at the direction of the Percales.

Cold reason blocked Matt's urge to pursue the men, trail them straight into the Percales' place, if need be. The night was far from over — and having failed — they would be back, this time most likely with reinforcements. The smart thing was to be ready — and waiting.

Moving swiftly, Matt brought the bay and stabled him inside the barn. Closing the door, he backtracked to the house where he took up a position on the porch where he was afforded a clear view of all the approaches, and there settled down. Hours later daylight found him drawn and worn, with a knife-like edge to his temper. Town Marshal Tinsley, riding up shortly after, found him thus.

"Figured this is where you'd be," the lawman said, climbing stiffly off his horse.

Sowers, eyes cold, dark spots in the flat planes of his face, considered the marshal with stolid disinterest.

"I reckon you meant what you said about staying," the lawman continued.

"My property. Aim to keep it . . . and I'll be obliged if you'll get off it," Sowers said flatly.

"Sure, sure," Tinsley said agreeably. "You seen anything of the Percales?"

"Tried burning down my barn earlier. Drove them off. Expect they'll be back."

"Can bet on it," Tinsley murmured, drawing up slightly.

Sowers caught the change in the lawman's eyes, the swift, unspoken warning. He rocked to one side, spinning and drawing his pistol in a single fluid motion. The crash of gunshots shattered the quiet, and again Matt Sowers was aware of bullets brushing by him. He saw one of the four riders who had come in from beyond the house topple backward, fall from his saddle. That would have been Tinsley's target. His own, dressed as were the others in long slickers and masks, had leaped from his floundering horse which had somehow got in the way of the bullet meant for its rider. Matt became aware then that Tinsley was on the ground, clutching at a spreading stain in his side — but there was no time to pause and help the lawman.

The remaining raiders were racing for the barn, and, wheeling, Sowers struck out in pursuit, firing as he went. The nearest of the masked men veered off, folding over his saddle, badly if not mortally wounded. The others hurried on, reached the bulking structure, and disappeared behind it. Sowers did not slacken his pace, and shortly also gained the building. He had not heard the pound of the horses as they continued on which could only mean the two had pulled up short, dismounted, and were now somewhere nearby.

Hugging the rough wall of the barn, Matt quickly made his way along it to the first corner. Pausing there, he let the tension flow out of his taut body, and his breathing slow. Then, gun ready, he stepped into the open. There was no one in sight. Moving fast, he crossed to the next corner of the structure, and then to the succeeding one, thus completely skirting it, finding no sign of the two men.

He was halfway along the front wall when he heard a single horse break into a run from behind the barn. It brought him to a stop, one horse — that meant that there was still a second man close by. A sound coming from inside the barn reached him. It could be the bay, but Sowers doubted the possibility. He had tied the horse securely in one of the stalls, and what he had heard appeared to come from deeper in the building.

Hurrying quietly, he reached the door of the barn, saw that it was partly open. Whoever it was, he definitely was inside. Matt remembered distinctly closing and latching the thick panel. Halting long enough to steady himself, Sowers flung the door aside, and lunged into the darkness for the safety of the first stall.

A flash of fire and thunderous blast met him halfway. He felt the searing heat of a bullet as it ripped across his ribs and, dropping to his knees, threw an answering shot at the spot where the slug had come from, filling the barn again with deafening echoes. The bay was plunging wildly about in fear, raising a whirl of dust to mingle with the powder smoke, but through it Matt could see the wavering figure of a man struggling to stay upright and lift the gun he clutched for another shot. The effort failed. Reflex action triggered the weapon, the report once more setting up echoes as the bullet drove harmlessly into the loose dirt of the building's floor. The man staggered forward, abruptly threw up his arms, and fell.

Cool, Matt reloaded his weapon and, continuing to hold it in his hand, moved away from the wall where he crouched, and crossed to the sprawled body. Rolling it over, he pulled off the mask. It was Shub Percale.

"Sowers? You all right?"

Tinsley's voice came from the doorway. Matt turned, feeling a weariness settle through him. "All right," he replied. "Shub Percale's in here . . . dead."

"His brother's laying out here along with one of their hired hands. Both dead, too. I reckon the fourth man got away."

"Doesn't matter," Sowers said, turning toward the door. "It's settled with the Percales . . ."

"Something that was their doing, not yours," the lawman said. He was pressing his folded bandanna to the wound in his side. "I'll be around to testify to that."

Hours later in his hotel room Matt Sowers paced restlessly back and forth. It was all over now, and there was nothing to hinder his going ahead with plans to rebuild the ranch, but somehow it no longer seemed important. He had won, yet there was no victory in the winning — only a vast sort of emptiness, and a future that offered nothing.

He paused, aware of footsteps in the hallway outside the door. It brought a surge of hope to him, and he waited and listened intently, scarcely breathing while he dared think who it might be. Somewhere a bell tolled, and the muffled *clop-clop* of a trotting horse drifted in from the street. The footsteps had ceased. Sowers, shrugging, turned away. It had been useless to believe . . .

A knock at the door brought him swiftly around. Crossing the room in two long strides, he jerked the panel open. Laurie was standing before him, and a wave of happiness swept through him.

"Oh, Matt!" she cried as she went into his outstretched arms. "I couldn't stay away! I . . ."

"And I was wrong not to tell you the truth about myself," he broke in. "But we'll talk about it another time. Right now I just want to hold you, and wash away the memory of the five years I've lost, and think about the future . . . our future."

A Gift for the General

The green-clothed hills of Virginia rolled away in soft, maiden curves to all directions. From a cloudless sky the midday sun impartially spread its radiance, formed deep pockets of shade where the trees and brush grew thick, bright splashes of light where there were open tracts, creating thereby a far-flung checkerboard of contrast. At the edge of one such clearing Sergeant-Major Davey Gooch, riding a broad-backed, long-eared mule, drew to a halt. He glanced questioningly at his companion, ancient, gray-whiskered Saul Hoxie who bestrode a bony little sorrel gelding.

"Yeah?"

"We best hold up h'yar for a bit," the old scout said. "And keep your talking down. They's bluebirds all around us." He squirmed about on the saddle, eased himself. Shifting the cud in his mouth, he cocked his grizzled head at the younger man. "One thing's been a-bothering me. How's it come you didn't say nothing to the other boys about this?"

"Needed somebody I could figure sharp on," Davey replied. "And somebody that could keep his mouth shut. Couldn't take no chance on the major hearing about it. You know what he'd a say . . ."

Davey Gooch let it ride with that. Smooth-faced, yellow-haired, in his middle twenties, he was young to be wearing the stripes of a sergeant-major. But there were many young men in John Mosby's 43rd Battalion of Confederate Rangers where rank depended upon ability and resourcefulness rather than seniority of years.

"Don't know if I ought to be proud or just plain have my head looked into," Hoxie said doubtfully, and spewed forth a stream of amber juice. "You ready to tell me what it's all about?"

"No time now," Davey said. "Let's move on."

"I allow as how we'd better set right where we are for a spell," Hoxie said. "There's a bluebird patrol coming this way."

Davey Gooch settled himself impatiently on the mule. He neither saw nor heard any evidence that would bear out Hoxie's prediction, but he would not question it. The old scout's ability to smell out Yankee soldiers was uncanny.

"When did you get this here notion you're so all-fired sot on?" Hoxie asked, biting off a fresh chew from a black square of tobacco.

"This morning," Davey said. "Was up on the ridge with General Jeb and the major. They were watching that Yankee camp, same as they do every day since the retreat . . ."

"Sure galls me!" Hoxie broke in, his voice heavy with disgust. "I'm mighty tired of just hanging around this neck of the woods. Not the way to be fighting Yankees, to my way of thinking."

"We ain't here to fight Yankees," Davey Gooch said, suddenly remembering he was of officer rank, "not this time, anyway. General Lee said we were to spy on that General Cronican and his regiments . . . nothing else. And the minute he starts to move out, we got to pass the word."

"Could just as easy be clipping off a few of them stray bluebirds, if the major'd let us! Be no harder than skinning a fat 'possum."

"The major's got his orders, same as we got ours. And with General Jeb hanging around, he ain't likely to go against them. The major always . . ."

"There's your Yank patrol," Hoxie murmured.

Davey Gooch shifted his gaze to the far side of the clearing. A platoon of Union infantry marched smartly into its center, led by a stocky, stiff-necked sergeant who marked his commands with the positive authority of many years' practice. The platoon reacted obediently; it wheeled, halted, started, about-faced, doubled ranked, wheeled again, and tramped on. A private stumbled on the uneven ground, recovered himself hurriedly to the vivid, fluent cursing of the non-com, rejoined the lockstep.

In silence the two Confederates watched the platoon cross the clearing, enter the trees on the far side, and disappear into the shadows.

"Just set tight," Hoxie said laconically. "They'll come a-traipsing back in a few minutes."

Davey plucked at the gray roach of the mule's mane. "You reckon a big general like Jeb Stuart ever gets lonesome, Saul? The way us regular soldiers do, I mean."

"Generals is human, same as the rest of us," Hoxie grunted. "Why?"

"That was what set me to figuring. Like I told you, I was up on the ridge this morning. I heard the general say he'd sure admire being home for his birthday, that a man ought to be with his woman and children and kinfolks at such time. He sounded sort of lonesome-like, even a mite homesick when he was talking."

"The general ain't been the same since that young 'un of his died last fall. Not that it's hurt his fighting none. Only, seems to me, he don't laugh so much, like he used to."

"Heard tell that little gal of his, Flora her name was, had been his favorite. Terrible shame."

"I reckon. But what's that got to do with us setting here in the middle of a whole bluebird army? Was the major to know this, he'd skin us alive!"

"He ain't going to know about it, leastwise not until it's all done with. You know that big white horse of that Yankee general's? The one that keeps winning all them races they hold at the camp every afternoon?"

"Sure do. That Yank's got a right to be proud as a turkey gobbler over that animal. He ain't lost a race yet."

"Well, two or three times I've heard General Jeb say as how he'd give a pretty penny to have that white for his very own."

"Mighty fine hoss," Hoxie admitted. "Sothron-bred and Sothron-growed, he ain't got no business belonging to no bluebird general. Wonder who he was stoled from?"

"That makes no difference to me," Sergeant-Major Gooch said. "I aim to steal him back."

Saul Hoxie, at that moment in the process of drenching a flat rock with a stream of brown juice, almost strangled. "What was that you said?"

"I figure to get that white horse."

"For the love of Gawd!" the old scout breathed feelingly. "That's what I thought you said."

"I'm going to give him to General Jeb for a birthday present, from us Rangers. Reckon that'll cheer him up some."

Hoxie wiped at his chin. "Be just a puny chore," he said, his tone dripping with sarcasm. "All we got to do is walk right into the middle of four, five regiments of bluebirds that ain't lost a skirmish in six months . . . and lead that hoss away."

"Way I got it figured, won't be so hard."

"It ain't going to be easy," Hoxie said, shifting on his saddle. "Them Yanks is restless as a covey of quail with a bull snake somewheres in the brush. Hold up . . . h'yar they come again."

The blue platoon marched into the clearing again. The men were sweating freely and the exposed portions of their skin glistened in the sunlight. Hoxie drew his revolver, took a practice aim.

"Sure would enjoy putting a ball right atwixt the eyes of that loud-mouthed sergeant. Could do it, too, right from where I'm setting."

"Don't you dare," Davey muttered. "We came after a horse, not a sergeant."

They watched the platoon execute its precise and tiring formations. Farther over to their right they could hear the sounds of the Union encampment — the faint shouts of other marching squads, the peaked, shrill notes of a bugler practicing on his horn, the clang of a regimental blacksmith working at his trade. Except for those remote, detached noises, the woods were quiet.

Back on the ridge Davey knew Mosby, with Jeb Stuart and the small band of Rangers who had accompanied them, would be observing the activities of the camp. They would be watching the comings and goings of couriers, the incessant drilling, the performing of tasks all soldiers must, of necessity, accomplish. And, like the Yankees, they would be awaiting the horse races, held daily, on the small, hastily built oval track that lay west of the encampment. It was the one break in an otherwise monotonous assignment for both factions that made the tedious hours bearable.

"Now," Saul Hoxie said after the Union platoon had tramped on out of the clearing, "just how you figure to do this here little easy job? Seeing as how it's my neck that's on the block with yourn, I got a feeling I ought to know."

"I got a plan," Davey said. "Like the major always told us, a man's got to have himself a plan before he can do anything. So I got mine. You think we can move on now? Time's getting short."

"Depends. Where you wanting to move to?"

54

"The far end of that race track. Where it runs through the trees."

The old scout studied Davey's square-jawed face for a few moments. He spat, grinned. "All right, boy. Follow me. But careful now. We'll be side-stepping bluebirds all through here, most likely."

They swung off through the brush, skirted the now empty clearing, keeping well within the fringe of dense growth. Fully aware of the danger of traveling deeply inside enemy territory, they proceeded with caution. But to men especially trained by John Mosby for such moments, they experienced little trouble. Like smoke shadows they circled the sprawling Union encampment, hearing the sounds of it rise and grow more distinct as they drew near, fade gradually as they passed the point directly opposite, and pushed beyond.

They continued on steadily through the brush and trees, followed out numerous shallow ravines and grassy swales, always avoiding the crests of bulging knolls until they came finally to a narrow roadway. Saul Hoxie lifted his heavy, veined hand, signaling a halt.

"Hyar's your race track," he said. "What's next?"

"Whereabouts on the track are we?" Davey asked.

Hoxie stood up in his stirrups, studied the surrounding country. "Halfway ... maybe three-quarters."

"Got to be at the end," Sergeant-Major Gooch said. "At the curve ... farthest from the starting gate."

Hoxie said nothing. He touched his pony with his heels, rode on. "Reckon you know every breath is putting us deeper into bluebird country."

"Sure I know it," Davey answered. "Never bothered you none before, though. Why you letting it eat on you now?"

" 'Cause always before I could do me some shooting, was it needful. You're telling me now that I can't."

"Maybe we won't have to."

"Meaning I can iffen some of them Yankees gets cute?"

"Meaning you can . . . if I tell you to."

A quarter hour later Hoxie again halted. "This'll be it."

Davey and the mule ambled out into the center of the track. Once it had been a wagon road but Cronican, the Union camp commander, flushed with a succession of victories and firmly convinced of his invincibility, had thrust the cares of war aside and now sought only relaxation, while he awaited new orders from headquarters.

Laboring soldiers had converted the roadway into a fairly decent racecourse, Davey saw. But at this point, the half circle at the end opposite the starting gate, there had been no convenient wagon trails to work with and the route had been slashed out of the brush and trees. Hard-running horses would necessarily have to slow their pace at this midway post. And, for that period of time they would be lost from view to the men back at the camp. It all suited Sergeant-Major Davey Gooch fine.

He returned to where Saul Hoxie waited patiently. "Race ought to be about starting," he said, glancing at the sun. "Might as well get ourselves set."

"Maybe I'm getting me an idea of what you're figuring to do," the scout replied. "You're going to let that white hoss come busting around the bend there and nab him. Which is fine. Only thing, when he don't show up along the track there in a little bit, them bluebirds are going to start wondering what happened and come running for a look-see. They'll be swarming about like yellow jackets. How we going to get by them?"

"Got that figured in my plan, too," Davey said. "Let's get back in the brush out of sight and I'll explain . . ."

A distant rifle shot cracked, clean and clear, through the still air.

"They're a-starting," Hoxie said.

"Good. We just made it. Now, watch sharp," Davey warned. He pulled off a short distance to where a decayed stump, well clothed with crêpe myrtle, offered an effective screen. "We don't do nothing unless that white horse is running."

But suddenly the white was there.

Davey Gooch saw the magnificent animal round the far turn in the track, head high, snowy mane and tail streaming in the breeze as he led his lone challenger handily. The young Ranger gasped softly in admiration. The white was a true champion, a Thoroughbred. He would stand at least seventeen hands high and tip the scales a good 1,200 pounds. And the way he ran — easily, joyfully — the muscles of his sleek body sliding and rippling beneath gleaming skin like a field of ripened grain shifting back and forth in a brisk wind!

His pink-lined ears were laid back and there was bold fire in his bulging eyes as though it infuriated him to be tested by a lesser opponent.

"*Hist*," Davey whispered. "When I sing out, we ride onto the track and stop them. And don't you be forgetting . . . no shooting."

Saul Hoxie grunted his answer. Davey waited until the horses with their crouched jockeys made the last turn, began to straighten out for the long back run.

"Now!" he said, and hammered the old mule in the ribs to get him onto the track.

Hoxie was at his side. They reached the center of the roadway together. The two soldiers, their faces blanched, sawed their mounts to a stop.

"Just set quiet," Davey said calmly, "and you won't get hurt none." He swung down, handed his pistol to Saul Hoxie. "Keep them covered whilst I get things ready."

He led the mule to where the white — a mare — minced nervously about on the dry turf. "Get off, Yank. You and me are trading."

"What?" the young soldier exclaimed incredulously.

"You heard him, bluebird," Hoxie said with a threatening wave of a pistol. "He's giving you a real genuine Missouri mule for that white horse. Now, you be doing just what he tells you to unless you want a bullet right through that pumpkin you're wearing for a head."

The Yankee came off the mare quickly. Davey took the reins, handed them to Hoxie. "You'll finish this here race, just like you started," he said to the soldier. "Only you'll be riding this mule. Climb aboard."

The Yank crawled onto the mule's gray back, seated himself on the saddle. Davey took one of several lengths of rope he had earlier provided and looped about his waist. He bound the soldier's wrists to the saddle. He moved then to the second man, who was silently watching from the bay he was riding. With a second piece of rope, he secured his hands, also. Both men were dressed lightly for racing and neither carried a weapon. There was no danger of their firing off an alarm, should they manage to work their hands free. But they could shout.

Davey strode back to the man on the mule. He reached up, seized the soldier's cotton shirt, and ripped it from his back. With it, he made gags and tied them tightly into place.

"Reckon they can finish the race now," he said, and stepped aside.

Saul Hoxie grinned. "That's a cute trick, boy. Them bluebirds back at camp won't have no idea something's happened until this pair reaches the finish line and starts yammering."

"You see now why I had to have me a white mule for this plan of mine," Davey said in a satisfied voice. He turned to the soldiers.

"Now, mind you, do just what I tell you! If you don't, my friend here is going to start using his pistol. You go on like nothing's happened. And you," he added, directing his words to the man on the bay, "you keep remembering the white is supposed to be winning so hold back. Let this here old mule keep ahead of you. You forget it and Saul here will sure remind you quick with a couple of bullets. You hear?"

The soldiers nodded sullenly. Davey strode to the mare. Standing beside the old scout's pony, she had calmed considerably, apparently discovering some kinship. The young Ranger swung to the saddle. He took his revolver from Hoxie's outstretched hand.

"All right," he said to the jockeys. "Get at your racing. And be mighty sure that mule wins."

The two contestants moved off down the track, the man on the mule flailing away with his heels on the unperturbed animal's ribs while the other soldier, mindful of Davey's warning, struggled to hold his horse behind. Within a few yards they broke into view of the waiting gallery at the camp. A faint cheer went up.

"Time we was leaving," Davey said. "Sure would like to stay and see for sure how that race turns out, but I reckon it ain't going to be too healthy around here."

They came up onto the ridge quietly a short time later. When they encountered the first of Mosby's pickets, they dismounted, continued on foot. They entered the camp, scarcely more than a dozen horses tethered to a rope stretched tightly between two trees, a small fire over which a sooty pot burbled and simmered, and a few scattered blanket rolls. Stuart and Mosby, with most of the Rangers, were gathered on the lip of the escarpment, a favored point from which to observe the Yankee camp. Saul Hoxie handed his mount to the horse holder, followed Davey as he led the mare to the top of the ridge.

At their approach Mosby turned. His thin-lipped mouth was set in a firm line but his sharp eyes showed surprise at sight of the big horse. Davey averted his face, avoided the Confederate major's questioning glance. He halted directly back of Stuart. The cavalry general's dress was always one to fire the imagination and now, even after a long week in improvised, inconvenient bivouac, the luster had not dimmed. His jacket was scrolled with glittering braid, laced with rows of shining buttons. The brim of his hat was doubled back, held in place with a gold star and the inevitable black ostrich plume rose proudly from its folds. He had laid aside his scarlet cape and the brilliant yellow sash around his waist was like a coil of encircling sunlight.

Davey Gooch, afraid of nothing, was, nevertheless, always a bit overawed by the splendor. He said: "General Jeb, sir . . ."

Stuart, watching the activities of the Union Army camp far below through a brass telescope, slapped his leg impatiently, roared: "Blast it all! Something's happened down there! Can't tell what! Never in my life saw a horse race like that one. Moved like they were pulling log sleds! And I'm not even sure it was that white mare that was running. Looked a little like a . . ."

He suddenly became aware that he had been addressed. He spun about. His broad forehead was corrugated by a frown. His thick mustache, curled up at the ends, and the luxurious, breast-length beard gave him the appearance of a fierce, 17th-century cavalier about to engage an opponent in a duel to the death.

"What was that . . . ?"

61

The commander of all the Confederate Army's cavalry forces halted in mid-sentence. His brilliant blue eyes widened as he beheld the mare. His lips parted in an abrupt gust of explosive breath. "How in the name of all that's holy did that horse . . . ?"

"General, sir," Davey Gooch began again, "I was hearing you saying something about your birthday. I . . . we . . . us Rangers, that is, would like to make you a present of this mare, knowing how much you admired her and such."

There was a long moment of silence. Farther over on the ridge Saul Hoxie, in a hoarse, whispering voice, was telling the remaining Rangers of the incident. Abruptly Jeb Stuart's great laugh broke across the hush. He stepped forward, slapped Davey Gooch on the shoulder.

"A birthday present!" he shouted. "You hear that, John? A birthday present of old peacock Cronican's prize horse!"

Stuart laughed until the tears ran down his ruddy cheeks, lost themselves in his vast beard. John Mosby, never a man taking easily to humor, joined in. There was no concealing the gleam of pride that began to glow in his eyes.

At last Stuart got control of himself. He laid his hand on Davey's shoulder. "What's your name, soldier?"

"Sergeant-Major David Gooch, sir."

"Well, Sergeant-Major David Gooch, I accept the fine birthday gift you have given me and I'll cherish it as long as I live. But tell me one thing . . . was that a mule you substituted for the mare down on the track?"

"Yes, sir," Davey said, and explained how the plan had worked.

Stuart began to laugh again. He staggered off to one side, plumped down on a stump, crossed his arms over his stomach, and rocked back and forth in helpless mirth. After a time he said: "I'd give a year's rations to have seen the look on Cronican's face when that mule came lumbering around the turn!"

Finally sober, Jeb Stuart got to his feet. He walked to where Davey Gooch stood beside the splendid mare. His broad face was serious now and there was more than kindness in his eyes.

"I thank you again, Sergeant-Major. And all the rest of you Rangers. This is the finest horse I ever laid eyes on and I'll ride her proudly in the name of the Forty-Third Battalion. God willing, she'll carry me forward in our march to victory."

"I figured you'd look mighty fine on her, sir," Davey murmured.

"I'll try to do justice to her beauty," Stuart said. "But there's one thing, Sergeant-Major, I don't think you realize. This is more than just a birthday gift. Knowing General Cronican for the pompous, prideful ass he is, I think, with that old gray mule, you probably just gained the most devastating psychological victory of the whole blasted campaign!"

Freight for Albermarle

by Dr. E. M. Clayton, M.D.
As told to Ray Hogan

The first time that I saw Bland, New Mexico, it was a booming silver-mining town of some 3,500 people. My brother and I pulled our buggy to a stop that summer afternoon in front of a place that had been pointed out as a hotel, but we soon found out that there wasn't a room to be had. In fact, beds were so scarce that men were sleeping in the streets or out under the trees on the side of the mountain, we were told by the clerk, but he directed us to the opposite end of town where a man had pitched a large tent and had placed some thirty or forty cots inside along the walls and down the center and was renting them for a dollar a night. We paid our fee and were glad to do it.

Since we had arrived late in the day, we didn't get any of our business attended to, my brother at that time being the representative for the firm now known as Dun & Bradstreet — and we didn't get much sleep that night, either, for the darkness was alive its entire length with men wandering around, yelling and shouting and raising hob in general. Most of them had come down into town after having spent the day at the Albermarle

Mine, back up the mountain, and they were really blowing off steam.

It took us all the next morning to complete our business, and then, since we didn't relish the long ride back to Albuquerque, we decided to spend another night in Bland and the afternoon just looking around, and thus get an early start next day. It must have been around three o'clock when one of Billy Trimble's freight wagons pulled in with some machinery equipment for Albermarle and we stood around, watching him hook up the "pusher" team in preparation for the hard climb to the mine.

It wasn't a good road in any sense of the word and Trimble's teamster, a Mr. Morgan, was taking no chances. He checked carefully all the harness and various parts of the heavy freight wagon and then, as a final precaution, obtained another team that he hitched ahead of his own bays.

In all he had six horses in leather, four pulling and two, rigged up in a sort of reverse harness, pushing from behind, and, just as he was ready to start, another wagon rolled in carrying a load of supplies and drawn by the largest span of mules I have ever seen. The wagon was out of Santa Fé and points east, and, when the driver saw Trimble's rig, he laughed and said: "Those sure must be puny horses you're driving!"

Mr. Morgan looked at the man. "They're all good horses, friend, and I aim to keep them good . . . and alive."

About twenty-five or thirty men had gathered around by this time, looking at the mules and listening to the talk, and the muleskinner looked at us and winked.

"I've always heard that two mules was better'n a half dozen horses. Guess this proves it."

"You ever pulled the hill to Albermarle?" Mr. Morgan asked.

The teamster shook his head. "Can't be any worse than a few others I've driven, and I've been driving back and forth from Independence for fifteen years."

"Well, take my advice and hitch on another team before you try this one," Mr. Morgan said and got ready to pull out.

"Wouldn't like to make a little bet on it, would you?" the muleskinner suggested.

Morgan shook his head. "No, and I'd advise you again to put a helper team with those mules."

But the teamster was deaf to Morgan's words and in a few minutes the crowd had taken up the idea and bets were being placed like wildfire, some for and some against the possibility of the mules pulling their load, unassisted, to the mine.

I had to admit that the mules certainly looked as if they could do it, if it could be done at all. They were magnificent animals, standing high and broad and powerful, and with the sun glistening down on their dark brown and black coats they looked almost like machines of some sort. But I knew Morgan was convinced that they could not do it, and I knew, also, that he was one of Trimble's best men and probably knew what he was talking about.

The wagers were finally all laid and the mule team pulled out and around Morgan and started up the long three-mile drag that wound around the mountain. We all trooped along behind, wading in the ankle-deep dust followed by Mr. Morgan and his teams some hundred yards or so back.

For the first mile the mules plodded steadily along, their thick bodies bent to the task and apparently in no strain while the teamster sat his seat and smoked on a big black cigar. But right after that point where the road cuts sharply back, the team began to labor a little. I could see them through the dust clouds, lying forward in the harness, heads thrust out and down as mules will do when the going gets hard.

The teamster, too, had come up from his seat and was standing, and I could hear the long blacksnake whip crack like a rifle every now and then. The mules dropped to a slow walk, and we soon caught up and were crowding along the sides of the wagon and close to the rear wheels. Morgan was maintaining his steady, deliberate pace, the horses pulling strong but not working too much.

And then quite suddenly it happened. I heard my brother say — "He's in trouble now for sure." — and I looked just as the wagon slid a little toward the edge of the road that was pretty bad there, rocky and slanting down and away from the mountain's side. One of the mules stumbled just then, caught itself, and lunged ahead, the teamster really plying the blacksnake and shouting so that the echoes were rolling back from the cañon below in a steady run.

This was the worst section of the road up from Bland and I heard Morgan shout, but I didn't catch it. I stood fascinated while the mules strained in the harness until I thought it surely would snap, and the wagon slowed and drifted gently toward the cliff. The 'skinner's whip cracked and cracked again, and the lathered animals fought to keep the big red wheels turning. It moved forward a slight bit, and then one of the mules went to its knees. The wagon slid to the edge, lurched against a rock, bounced up, and went over the side, dragging the team and driver with it.

I heard the mules scream, mingling with the yell of the teamster and the clattering of the wagon and its load as it crashed and slammed against the rocks and trees. For a long minute we all just stood there, too surprised to move, and then all at once we poured over the edge and down into the bottom of the cañon. But there wasn't a great deal we could do. The driver was badly hurt, one mule was dead of a broken neck, and another so injured that it had to be put out of its misery. The load was a total loss.

I glanced back up the slope in time to see Mr. Morgan and his team just topping the rise of the hard pull, not hurrying, not stopping, but just moving steadily along, and I thought of that old saw — "A man knows what he knows." — and I realized then that Billy Trimble's man certainly knew what he was talking about.

I drove up to Bland not long ago, but there is no raucous glory there now. There are only the sagging remnants of shacks with empty windows for hollow eyes and trees struggling through doors where men once passed. Nature has reclaimed the area once wrested from the steep hillsides and now only the pines and piñons and spruce and lesser growth stand where once a crowded street cut its way. As to the Albermarle, I made no effort to locate the once active and prosperous mine, for it, too, I realized would be nothing but a ghost of rotting wood and rusting steel and sightless, square eyes. And sometimes it's better if you don't remember things as they are but rather as they have been . . .

The Man Who Wore the Star

Everyone in Catron knew John Wescott, and yet nobody really knew him. Now, as he stalked slowly down the middle of the street in the late afternoon's breathless heat, they watched him going about the business they had hired him to do in that grim, matter-of-fact way they had come to associate with him. They were aware that he had come to their small town, which was on the New Mexico-Oklahoma border, in response to a need for a sheriff. He came without a wife but had brought his five-year-old son, called Danny, and had rented the old Younger place at the edge of town. He was a serious, close-lipped man, seemingly alive only to the boy and to the job of keeping law and order. Beyond that they knew nothing.

He was tall and looked it despite the flat-crowned hat pulled low on his head, accentuating the angularity of his lean face. A black string tie closed the collar of his white shirt, which he always wore neatly cuffed, and the faint whispering of his gray cord trousers was plainly audible in the dead silence of the narrow, dusty street as he strode on methodically.

Somewhere near the Cattleman's Bank a stray shaft of sunlight, thrusting its way between two closely spaced buildings, caught him and glittered briefly upon the star pinned to his left breast. Good target, he thought, but there was no break in his stride, for it was not in the make-up of John Wescott to dwell greatly upon the uneven streaks of luck that befell a man. To him it was an old pattern, varied by circumstances but governed eternally by the changeless objective — the lawbreaker.

A horse at the rail in front of the hotel whinnied nervously in the strained quiet, and Wescott slowed a little as the distance to Diamond's Livery Barn lessened. Imperceptibly his hand dropped, his long fingers brushing the butt of the gun hanging at his hip. The gap was only a score of yards when he came to a full stop and carefully considered the squat, rambling, frame building with half-shut eyes.

"Come out, Anson!" he called, his voice bouncing against the fronts of nearby structures and resounding hollowly. "Come out with your hands up!"

A long minute dragged by filled only with the faraway barking of a dog. Then a man, bent low, plunged into the open from behind the barn, the gun in his hand crackling.

A bullet thudded into Wescott's arm, high above the elbow, and drove him backward a step. But even as he staggered, his own pistol was out, laying its flat echoes twice along the length of the street. The man called Anson pitched forward on his face.

Momentarily the world of dust and bright sunlight and gray buildings seemed to be suspended, peopled only by two figures, one upright, one prone, and then suddenly windows were slamming up, doors were opening, and men were rushing into the street.

"Get the coroner," Wescott said to the first ones who reached him and, wheeling, walked steadily to the office of old Doc Mitchell, who was waiting for him.

The reward for Red Anson, murderer, dead, was ample, and it arrived on the Butterfield stage a short month later. Wescott, standing on the boardwalk in front of the Horton Hotel, received the long envelope bearing the seal of the territorial governor, opened it, smiled up at the driver and the deputy who rode shotgun, and tucked it inside his shirt. There he stopped, a change coming over the man, stiffening him, draining the color from his face as a woman stepped down from the coach.

Their eyes locked, hers steady under the hard, direct gaze of Wescott's, and a word formed on her lips. No sound came, however, and whatever it was died there unuttered. A look of hopefulness crossed her features, and, turning, she entered the hotel. Wescott followed at once, catching up with her in the lobby.

"How did you know?" he said, placing himself in front of her, blocking her. His voice was low, and the question was that of a man who, thinking himself well hidden from the world, suddenly finds himself discovered.

"Anson, of course. That kind of news traveled fast."

At the sound of her voice, Wescott shuddered inwardly, a flood of memories washing through him. He had eaten his heart out a thousand times remembering her voice, the way her dark hair piled up around her face, her soft skin, and her gray eyes. But that was all over now, all behind him.

"I warned you last time never to follow us again," he said.

"Never is a long time," she said slowly. "Too long. Can't you see by now," she added, her voice rising on a note of desperation, "that you can't keep him from me? I'll follow you to the end of the earth if it's only for a glimpse of him now and then."

"You made your choice . . . ," Wescott began.

"I know . . . I know, and I've paid a thousand times for my mistake, John. Must I go on forever doing it?"

"You made the choice, Clarissa," he repeated softly. "You went with Kemp of your own mind."

"Does he . . . does Danny know about me?" she asked then.

"He thinks you're dead. Better that way."

"Dead," she echoed wearily, eyes straying toward the single, dirt-streaked window. Elsewhere in the hotel men moved about, a bell rang, and from the kitchen in the back came the rattle of dishes. "It couldn't be worse."

"Stay away from the boy. He is not to know."

Clarissa Wescott nodded dumbly. "He is not to know," she repeated mechanically. "But I *will* see him!" she added, turning back suddenly. "You can't keep me from that, and, if you leave again, I'll follow you again, just as I have done before, and I'll keep on following you as long as I'm able."

Wescott considered her words while the recollections of a half dozen towns, a half dozen dusty, sun-baked roads, and as many hurried, night-time flights trailed across his mind. None had brought a solution, and the problem had returned each time to taunt him. A measure of the bound-in bitterness welled up in the man then, sharpening his words, coloring them with a tinge of sarcasm.

"Always remember, it was your bargain."

Her shoulders sagged and she let her eyes fall. "Is there no forgiveness in you at all?" she murmured.

John Wescott shrugged. "You left me and your son for another man. Is that something that can be forgiven?"

Pivoting, he walked across the shadowy lobby with its wall adornments of time-worn pictures and cobwebby deer heads and went out into the street.

The hours turned long for Wescott after that. Time that usually moved swiftly with the performing of everyday chores suddenly was an irksome, boring thing filled with bits of conversation, heated words, and thinly veiled threats, and through it all ran a thin current of doubt and indecision.

It was near the end of the week, when he was carrying on a desultory conversation in the doorway of his office with jailer Latch Sebring, that his restless vision caught sight of Danny trotting down the street, indulging himself in one of his periodic exploring trips.

Amused, Wescott watched as the boy tarried before Crossman's window, moved on to the next, and then crossed over, headed apparently for the hotel. He knew Danny's love for the framed prints and mounted animal heads displayed there, but only in that moment did he think of the possibilities should Clarissa be present.

His first impulse, strong and angry, was to intercept the boy and eliminate any chance meeting between the two. Then he recognized and admitted the futility of such action. He could not rightfully expect Danny to grow up isolated by him to suit his own standards.

Irritated and disturbed by his own discovery, he turned to his horse, swung into the saddle, and rode off toward the short hills.

That night John Westcott listened to an excited Danny telling him of a nice lady who had bought him a dish of ice cream while he was at the hotel. He watched the light dance in the boy's eyes as he related the incident, and old uncertainties crowded into his mind again, filling him with a sort of fear and helplessness.

"She knows you, too," Danny finished up.

"That so?" Wescott said, keeping his voice even.

The boy nodded, proud of the moment. "I told her my name and that you was the sheriff, and she said she had heard of you."

"That's fine, Son," Wescott murmured, feeling relief run through him like cold water. "Now you better hit for bed."

"Yes, sir, only I been thinking. She'd make a nice mother."

★ ★ ★

The next day Will Kemp came into town riding the big gray horse he had owned while he was foreman at Stratton's Diamond S in faraway Wyoming.

Wescott was standing before his office, and a visible change came over the man as his eyes followed Kemp to the rail at the hotel, watched him dismount, tie up, and enter. He remained there, as he had been, quiet and expressionless, but the tight, small lines that gathered at the corners of his lips were evidence of the turmoil that Kemp's arrival had released within him.

He had not changed position when, a few minutes later, Kemp came back through the hotel's door and walked the short distance to him.

In the brief time it took the man to cover the short yards, Wescott's eyes took him in completely, noting with some satisfaction the haggardness of his face, his ill-kempt appearance, and the general looseness of the man. This was a far cry from the proud, dashing Will Kemp who had first entered his life; this was a worn and disillusioned Will Kemp, uprooted and driven weary by his own desires and now turned desperate. He came to a stop ten paces away.

"I've come a long way to talk to you," he said.

Wescott shook his head. "We've got nothing to talk about."

Kemp ignored the words. "Give Clarissa the boy. There'll be no peace with her until she has him. You hear? Let her have him!"

Suddenly the moment became charged and breathless, and the feel of impending action hung in the air. A half dozen people appeared from nowhere at the sound of Kemp's lifted voice, and as quickly vanished. From inside the jail Latch Sebring's words came querulously: "What's the matter out there?"

"Get out of town," Wescott said slowly, his tone dry as winter leaves. "Get out, Will, before there's trouble."

Kemp shook his head. "Half a woman is no woman at all. I haven't spent a decent hour with her since the night you blew Laramie with the kid. There's no satisfaction this way and it's in my mind to change it. She wants him, and I mean to see she gets him. You understand?"

"Get out," Wescott repeated, spacing the words distinctly.

Kemp studied him momentarily, apparently judging his temper, then glanced at Sebring, standing now in the doorway of the jail.

"Reckon that leaves only one answer," he said. "Next time we meet, be ready."

Turning on a heel, he moved back to his horse, mounted, and rode out of sight beyond Diamond's Livery Barn.

John Wescott was essentially a fatalist. It came with the life he had chosen, and his constant proximity to sudden death had long since ceased to trouble him. He simply lived each day as a man prepared every moment for a supreme test and confident in his own ability. For that reason, Will Kemp's threat scarcely touched his thinking.

He sat now, silent and moody, on the front porch of his home, watching a yellow moon lift from behind the low, rolling hills to the east. Like a man, he mused, being born and growing and getting stronger and finally standing tall and complete, and then the slow, inevitable trip down the other side to nothingness.

But a man could leave something. He could leave some good memories and perhaps a legend or two that would increase with the telling. More important, he could leave a legacy of honesty to his son, the kind of honesty that spares no personal feelings.

His thoughts turned to Danny and then, swiftly, to Clarissa, and he became conscious of the old, dull ache gnawing at his insides. He had driven himself to abide by a woman's decision, fiercely compelling her to live by her choice and, paradoxically, was tormented by his own actions.

On this night, however, all his doubts crystallized and he was forced to admit that he had been wrong. It was Clarissa, Kemp, and the boy. It could not logically be any other way, and he could not possibly expect to change it. John Wescott made his decision.

Near midnight he roused from his chair, paused to listen to a coyote throwing its lonely challenge across the silvery shine of the mesa, and then retired to his bed.

The morning was well started when he reached his office, and he stood outside for a time, watching with detached interest as three riders loped out of town toward the west. He had his moment of regret then, for Catron had not been like other places. Here he had felt the urgency to send down and firmly anchor his roots, but a man did what had to be done and made the best of it.

Slowly, almost reluctantly, he let his gaze drift along the narrow, dusty street with its tall, false-fronted buildings that were already beginning to trap the day's heat and sounds and smells. At that moment he saw Clarissa walk out onto the porch of the hotel, speak briefly to a man loitering there, and then go back in.

Wescott shrugged, turned inside, and for the next few minutes busied himself with writing out a resignation which he placed in an envelope, sealed, and laid in a prominent place. After that, he carried a few personal belongings to his horse, stuffed them in the bags of the saddle, secured his slicker behind the cantle, and then moved slowly back to the doorway.

" 'Morning," Sebring said at his elbow. "Sure is a nice morning."

Wescott nodded, turning aside to let the jailer enter. He waited until the man had completed his usual business of standing his rifle in the corner rack, strapping on his handgun, and opening the windows. Then he said: "Latch, I want you to do me a favor."

"Yeah?"

"You know that woman that's stopping over at the hotel? I want you to give her a message for me."

The jailer looked at Wescott with interest. "That so? What?"

"Go down there now and tell her I said she could have both of them. I'm pulling out."

"What?" Sebring said, not understanding.

"Just tell her I said she could have both of them. She'll know what I mean."

The jailer stared at him with wonder in his eyes, but Wescott turned away. He waited for a time, listening to Sebring's grumbling, and then, as the man's footsteps died away, he smiled, finding some amusement in Sebring's mystification.

Remembering the star, he unpinned it, and fastened it to the envelope on the desk. After that, he remained silent, staring at the bit of nickel as if trying to understand his own actions more fully. Discovering it or not, he sighed, glanced around the small room, wheeled, and walked out into the street to his horse.

From the saddle he looked west to the small dust cloud that would be the three riders he had seen earlier in the day. That was his destination, too — whatever lay beyond the low wall of purple on the other side of the Sierras.

He sensed that someone was near him. Nettled by his own slowness and thinking that Sebring had already returned from his errand, he pulled the horse around sharply. Will Kemp's figure, blocky and grim, faced him a dozen paces away.

"You ready?"

There was no reason in Kemp's bloodshot eyes, only an insane hardness that told of hours and days and months of bitter frustration that had at last driven him to violent action.

"I am," Wescott said. All his careful planning dissolved in that moment, leaving him stranded, at bay, unwilling to play his hand in this deadly game. But the make-up of the man kept him silent.

"You getting down off that horse?" Kemp pressed, his body a tense, coiled spring in the slanting light.

Wescott nodded. Turning the horse broadside, he slid from the saddle, keeping the animal between them. Both feet on the ground and in balance, he slapped the buckskin's rump, driving him aside. "There's no call for this," Wescott said then. "I'm pulling out."

Kemp laughed harshly. "You'd be back in a month, changing your mind. It's you or me . . . now."

"Killing's no answer, but if that's what you want, I'm here."

He stood quietly, waiting, both legs stiff, hands hanging loosely at his sides. Vaguely he was aware of people in the street, of voices, of a woman's voice, but he shut them all out, concentrating from experience on the job that was at hand. In his business it was only the quick who remained alive. Then suddenly John Wescott knew that this was the one time when he must not be counted among the quick. "Your move," he said.

The silence ran on, heavy, oppressive, broken again by the woman, nearer now. Wescott waited, watching for Kemp's first move, for that swift, upward sweep of his arm that would spell the finish of the long, lonely trail. The woman's voice, high with hysteria, dinned at him, lashing at his consciousness.

"No . . . no, John! Can't I make you understand! It's you . . . not him, John! *You!*"

The words reached Wescott then, broke through the cloak of insensibility that had surrounded him into his intent mind. A surge of feeling swept through him, awakening him, drawing his attention for the briefest of moments. That was when Kemp made his move.

Even as he dragged at his own gun, Wescott saw the pistol bloom in Kemp's hand and felt the solid smash of the bullet into his side. It spun him around, but the old coolness had returned, and his own weapon made its sharp reply. Kemp staggered back, hit squarely in the chest.

Dimly Wescott remembered, completing the slow twist, holding his gun up, and then he knew he was falling.

Clarissa was crying in his ear: "Oh, John, won't you ever understand? It has always been you . . . you and Danny ever since that first day and I realized I had made a mistake . . . you and Danny and me . . . nobody else."

Then he heard Doc Mitchell's voice, and felt gentle hands probe under his shirt. "He'll do. Nothing but meat. He's a lucky one . . . every time it's been in the meat."

Latch Sebring said: "Reckon I'd better pin this star back on him, seeing as how he's going to keep on wearing it."

Wescott, they saw, was smiling.

One More Hill to Hell

Dan Grimshaw sat quietly in his saddle, a high, square shape in the faint light. His lean face was set, a smooth gravity laying its stillness over his features while his eyes probed thoroughly the scattering of poor buildings of the run-down homestead. About him and all around him a spring dawn was flooding down from the hills to the east, spreading swiftly over the prairie, tinting the grass purple, and changing the land to a restless sea of color.

"Tough," he murmured. "Tough for a woman."

He shrugged then, something in him seeming to crystallize, forcing him to a decision.

"Miz Olmstead!" he called out.

The door of the small frame shack flung back at once and Melissa Olmstead stood in the opening. Lamplight was a yellow glow behind her and the morning's soft wind pressed its gentleness against her dress, molding it to her figure in sharp relief. The mass of dark hair that Grimshaw had noted before, when on occasion he had passed the place and seen her in the yard, was a glinting halo about the pale oval of her face.

She was thoroughly womanly, cut to move a man deeply, and Grimshaw was immediately aware of Caine

Pomeroy's reasons for friendly overtures and his gloved treatment in evicting her from Kingpin range. His treatment of other homesteaders had been less tolerant — ruthless, brutal raids in the night, fire, gun play — and in the end they had all drifted on, broken and defeated, unable to withstand Kingpin's merciless power and far-reaching influence.

All, that is, but Melissa Olmstead who, perhaps, after the death of her husband had less reason to stay than any. Alone she had remained, stubbornly refusing Pomeroy's offers, facing him as she faced Grimshaw now, bitter, defiant, and with an old carbine rifle held firmly in her hands.

"Well?" she said coolly.

"'Morning," Grimshaw answered, touching his wide hat.

"If you've come with some message from Pomeroy, you can save your breath."

Grimshaw shifted in the saddle, the silence becoming thickly uncomfortable between them after that. In the shed behind the house a horse stamped and blew noisily and a flock of crows, settling in the lower, untended field, flung their harsh cries into the gathering day.

"Pomeroy don't know anything about this," Grimshaw said at last. "I'm here as a friend."

"Friend?" Melissa echoed. "You're Kingpin, aren't you?"

He shook his head. "That's neither here nor there now. Take my advice and clear out today. Go back to your people. Pomeroy's through waiting."

Melissa's eyes flicked him with surprised interest, but suspicion had its strong way with her.

"Is that your advice . . . or Pomeroy's?"

Again Grimshaw shrugged, biting down the impatience that plucked at his lips. "I'm telling you as a friend . . . get off Pomeroy's range. I'm through at Kingpin. I'm moving on."

"Drifter," she murmured half aloud. Then: "What's the matter? Got your fill of seeing honest men beaten, whipped, killed, and run off their own land?"

Bitterness welled and surged through her words as the wounds reopened and Grimshaw could see the brave defiance and determination momentarily crumple on her face.

"Go back to your people," he said then kindly, a softness in him deepening his words. "There's nothing ahead of you now but trouble if you stay."

Abruptly he touched his hat and, wheeling about, cut toward the shallow valley where a winding stand of willows marked the broken, irregular course of the Shannin.

Reaching the stream, he dismounted, ground-reined the buckskin horse, and, taking a small lard bucket from his saddlebags, dipped up a bit of the clear water. He started a small fire. Placing the bucket over it, he sat back, waiting for it to boil.

He heard then the steady drum of a running horse and a tight furrow crowded his brow as he wondered upon it. The sound died, and, the water reaching its peak, he poured a handful of coffee into the bucket, watched the liquid rise, and then set it off, stirring

85

down the froth with a twig. After it had cooled a bit, he lifted it to his mouth and drank deeply of the steaming brew.

The day's full-blown heat had begun to lay across the prairie by the time he was again in the saddle, and he pulled his hat lower against the rising glare. For a time he followed the Shannin, catching what he could of its vagrant coolness and letting his mind run back over Melissa Olmstead's words. He hoped she would take his suggestion and leave her small land holdings to Pomeroy, but he could not find it in his mind to blame her if she did not. After all, he was a Kingpin rider and she had no understanding of his thoughts.

Near noon he cut away from the valley and climbed the short hills toward Kingpin's main headquarters, lying in the flat hollow of the Crude country. He paused briefly on the last crest, letting his eyes drift over the vast, rolling domain of Caine Pomeroy and he had a short moment of understanding for this cattleman's problem — grass was gold in this arid land which, once broken by the plow, went to dry dust under the summer's driving sun — but he could find no final justification for Pomeroy even in that thought. Suddenly anxious to get a bad chore over, he spurred the buckskin into a gallop, rode a few minutes later into Kingpin's yard, and pulled up before the rack of the bunkhouse.

He sat for a moment in the saddle, a feeling of something amiss running through his long frame. When he dismounted, he was conscious of a small tension building itself along his nerves, turning him wary. But there was no outward change in him as he looped the reins over the rack bar and walked the short distance to the main house where Pomeroy lived. He strode across the porch that ran the full length of the building, pulled open the screen door, and stepped into the front room, used by Kingpin's owner as an office.

Pomeroy was there, sitting behind the table made to serve as a desk, a long cigar uptilted in his small mouth, the sly malevolence of power lying boldly across his dark face. Behind him stood Britt Whitcomb, Kingpin's foreman, beloved of no man or woman and with no redeeming qualities in his nature but an unbounded devotion to Pomeroy and Kingpin. Two other riders, Alvy Ryan and a man named Joe Siddons, lounged in opposite corners of the room. Little flags of danger were sounding their warnings to Grimshaw then. He nodded briefly in greeting.

"Little early for you to come in," Pomeroy observed dryly.

"I'm quitting," Grimshaw said. "Like to draw what money I have coming."

"Why, now, that's right interesting," Pomeroy ran on in his mocking voice. "Especially when Britt here tells me he overheard you giving the little nester widow a little advice early this morning. Good advice, too."

Grimshaw stood quietly. He felt then, rather than heard, the fifth man in the room, standing in the corner behind him. And he remembered suddenly the sound of the running horse he had heard when he was making coffee early in the day. That must have been Whitcomb.

"One thing that bothers me, though," Pomeroy said after a time. "What's your angle? You're no nester."

"Maybe," Grimshaw said in a voice as dry as winter grass, "I don't like to see people pushed around."

"Don't worry about that, friend," Pomeroy said then. "Nobody is going to push that young widow around. I'm simply clearing my range and inviting her to come here, say, as my housekeeper."

Grimshaw's answer was brief. "Touch that girl and I'll kill you."

Caine Pomeroy eyed the tall rider thoughtfully. "You would at that," he mumbled. "Too bad. I like your kind and I could use you here on the ranch. But until I get my other troubles cleared, I expect I'd better fire you, and keep you here as my guest. Then I'll decide what's for you." Abruptly Pomeroy's bland casualness dropped away. "Take him to the old bunkhouse and keep a guard on him. If he tries to break out, cut him down."

Grimshaw felt the hard muzzle of a gun jam into his back. Siddons and Ryan stepped forward and relieved him of his pistol.

"Let's go," Ryan said, and kicked back the door.

Grimshaw turned, hearing Whitcomb's voice make its complaint: "Caine, about that widow. Now, we don't want no woman around here."

"Who asked you?" Pomeroy snapped.

"Means nothing but trouble. Just trouble," the foreman continued. "Just trouble."

The old bunkhouse was a small, one-roomed affair, abandoned some years back for the new structure which stood close by. It was completely barren except for a wooden bench running across one end, and Grimshaw, entering, sat down and watched as Ryan pulled the door shut. He arose then and slammed up the window over the bench. Instantly Ryan was there, gun in hand.

"Hot in here," Grimshaw said and sat back down.

"Now, you heard what Caine said," Ryan warned. "Any foolishness and you're a dead man. Just behave until tomorrow, and then likely he'll send you on your way."

"Why tomorrow?" Grimshaw asked.

"Because . . . ," Ryan began and caught himself suddenly. "I'm telling you nothing," he snapped. "You'll find out in time."

He turned then and watched as Siddons came across the yard bringing a plate of beans and meat and a tin cup of coffee. Gun still ready, he waited while the man set them on the bench, and Grimshaw, finding himself hungry, ate his fill. Afterward, he stretched out full length on the bench and slept, knowing that little, if anything, could be done until after dark. Awakening near sundown to the *clang* of the supper triangle, he arose, stretched the stiffness from his muscles, and checked the yard from the window.

Smoke was curling up from the kitchen stack into the fading light and the night's sharp chill was beginning to settle over the valley. Ryan had exchanged guard duty with Siddons who sat, back to the wall of the new bunkhouse, facing the door to Grimshaw's cell. A half dozen horses stood hipshot at the rack, and Grimshaw mentally observed: *Three missing . . .*

A few minutes later Ryan brought him his evening meal — meat, beans, and coffee again — and placed it on the bench under Siddons's watchful eyes.

"Leave the door open," Grimshaw said then, trying to judge the temper of the pair. "Hot in here. I'm not going anywhere with you standing there with that gun in your hand."

Ryan stared at him for a moment. "Seems cool enough to me," he said, but he left the door wide. "Get your grub." He nodded to Siddons. "I'll watch him."

Grimshaw finished the plate and strolled to the door, coffee in hand. He sipped it slowly, making it last, and, when it was gone, he asked conversationally: "Been with Pomeroy long?"

Ryan waited a moment. Then: "Year or so, I reckon."

"Big outfit. That what made you sign on?"

Ryan grunted. "One job's as good as another."

Grimshaw shook his head. "I won't buy that, Alvy. A man's got to live with himself, and, if he's working for an outfit like Kingpin, there's going to be a lot of things in his head that bother him. Things that could make him look down his own gun barrel to forget them."

"Nobody bucks Pomeroy," Ryan said. "He's the power in this country and nobody moves unless it's all right with him."

"Not good," Grimshaw said, watching the man closely.

"Gets what he wants just the same," Ryan insisted, his voice lifting a little.

"Maybe so, but there'll come a day when he'll push the wrong man and that will be the end of him. It always happens sooner or later and it don't matter how big the big man is, he'll be just as dead."

"So?" Ryan said cautiously.

"You ever wonder what happens to the men who have been doing the dirty work for him? Their protection's gone then and there's no big man to throw his weight around and keep the rest of the little people from taking them apart. They aren't afraid then, Alvy, and they start remembering old scores that have to be settled."

"And what do they do then?" Britt Whitcomb's voice said from the darkness beyond Ryan. "What happens then, mister?"

The foreman moved in beside Ryan and set a coal-oil lamp on the ground next to him. "Here, you can light this if you need it," he said. "You're doing a lot of talking for a man on a tight rope," he said to Grimshaw. "Maybe you'd like to tell me a few things, too."

The edge on the man's tone rubbed into Grimshaw. Whitcomb had always irritated him and the mere sight of the slight, hatchet-faced man with his close-set eyes was enough to rankle him. A match flared in the darkness, and Ryan touched the lamp's wick, filling the narrow corridor between the two bunkhouses with yellow light.

"I could tell you a lot of things," Grimshaw said, "all of which wouldn't sound very pretty to you."

Whitcomb stepped in close. "You're long on talk, drifter, but short on everything else. I told Caine you

91

were a four-flusher when he hired you. I can name a
few more things right quick."

Grimshaw's driving blow came out of the semidarkness and, missing the point of the jaw, connected
farther back, and Whitcomb slammed back against the
bunkhouse wall. The wind went out of the man in a
gust, his hat flew off and rolled drunkenly away, and his
pistol, jarred from its scabbard, fell to the ground.

Ryan was on his feet instantly, gun drawn, but
Grimshaw stood quietly, rubbing his knuckles. He
watched the foreman rise slowly. The hatred in
Whitcomb's eyes was fire itself and for a long moment
he stared at Grimshaw while fury plucked and tugged
at the corners of his thin lips. And then, saying nothing,
he picked up his gun, retrieved his hat, and walked off
into the gloom.

"Now that was a fool thing to do," Ryan said, settling
back down. "You're good as dead."

Grimshaw smiled, moving back into the room.
"Maybe," he said, and began to pace the small quarters
restlessly. He could feel Ryan's eyes upon him, hard
and suspicious, but he knew there was doubt in the
man's mind, too, and it pleased him to have it that way.
Ryan would do a little deep thinking in those next few
hours.

"Going to be a long night," he observed then, and
stretched out on the bench again.

He could hear Ryan's grumbling reply. The clatter of
dish-washing chores came from the kitchen of the main
house, and one of the ranch dogs set up a monotonous
yapping that carried hollowly out into the prairie.

Evening faded into darkness, starlight strengthened, and the many shadows laid their irregular shapes upon the land. A door slammed, and Siddons clumped across the hard pack. Grimshaw could hear the low murmur of voices. After a time one — Siddons or Ryan, he could not tell which — returned to the main house.

Minutes later Grimshaw heard the door bang again and the sounds of men mounting to leather and then the steady pound of horses as they left the yard in a rush. Raising his head cautiously, he looked through the window. Two horses remained at the rack, his and one other.

"Ryan!" he called, keeping his voice level.

"Ryan's gone," Siddons said. "What you want?"

"Sure like a smoke," Grimshaw said. Desire for action was sweeping him, urgent and demanding and unyielding, for, understanding the devious ways of some men, he knew that Pomeroy would strike that night if Melissa Olmstead had not accepted his advice. A tremor of anger went through him and there was a moment while he cursed all men such as Caine Pomeroy. But his voice was controlled and even as he said: "Need a light. Mind if I come out and use your lamp?"

Siddons considered for a time. "Come ahead," he said finally. "But no monkeyshines!"

Grimshaw strolled through the doorway, rolling a cigarette. Stopping momentarily, he breathed deeply of the night's coolness, taking a quick re-check of the horses as he paused. Satisfied, he moved on.

"Get your light and get back inside," Siddons ordered irritably.

Grimshaw bent for the lamp. Tipping it sidewise, he caught up the funnel of heat from the chimney and the cigarette glowed into life. Drawing in a deep lungful, he exhaled smoke slowly, and then in a single movement flung the lamp straight at Siddons and lunged away.

Siddons's gun exploded into the silence and Grimshaw felt the searing burn of the bullet as it drove through the fleshy part of his thigh and spun him half around. It sent him off balance momentarily, but he crashed full weight into Siddons and they went down, rolling in the spreading flames. Grimshaw clawed at the gun and wrenched it away, and, as they swayed to their feet, struggling for its possession, he brought up his knee hard into Siddons's belly, and the man gasped and buckled. Grimshaw drove him to the ground with a blow to the ear.

Siddons came up unsteadily, and again Grimshaw dropped him with a hard fist. The man stiffened and lay still.

Sucking for breath, Grimshaw dragged him beyond reach of the fire and beat out the smoldering places on their clothing. Feeling then the sharp lance of pain in his leg, he wasted a minute while he bound the wound with his handkerchief, and then, half running, half walking, he reached the buckskin and swung up into the saddle and turned the horse about. Looking back once, he could see the fire spreading and caught a glimpse of the Chinese cook, peering out of a window in complete fright. Then he put the horse out of the yard and into the short hills at a dead gallop.

He saw the yellow-red glow hanging in the sky long before he topped the last rise and knew at once that he had been right in his calculations. The Olmstead place was burning, and he had his moment of hope that Melissa was not there, that she was gone, on her way back to wherever she had come from. But he felt no assurance and he knew the fact was something that must be settled in his own mind.

He had cut himself into this deal primarily because of a desire to see the right thing done, but somewhere it had stopped being a matter of objective consideration. He thought of the girl, as he had last seen her, and he remembered Caine Pomeroy's words and a coldness settled over him, turning him still, wiping the excitement from him and replacing it with a suppressed sort of fury. He swung away from the crest of the rise then, running the buckskin slowly until he crossed the dully sparkling water of the Shannin. He resumed the fast pace then along the spongy banks until at last he came to the point where he was nearest and just below the Olmstead place.

The house was a tower of crackling flames. The barn was a smoking ruin, but two or three small outbuildings yet stood, small blocks of darkness against the fire's color. Remaining in the concealment of the willows, Grimshaw could see Pomeroy and the rest of Kingpin milling about in the brilliantly lit yard, but there was no sign of the girl, and hope once again lifted within him. He recognized then the necessity for getting closer if he was to be certain, and, bending low over the buckskin's neck, he worked his way along the shallow draw that footed the homestead, to a point where it curved in closest and then moved swiftly in.

Luck was with him and he checked the horse at an outsize juniper and swung stiffly from the saddle. His bad leg gave away, and he clung to the saddle for a moment while the pain raced through him, and then slowly ebbed. Afterward, he secured the horse and, favoring the injured thigh, moved in a dozen more yards to another growth of juniper.

This reached, he discovered that he still could not see or hear distinctly Pomeroy and his riders and, dropping flat on his belly, wormed his way toward a small tool shed standing somewhat to the side of the main house. Every movement in that prone position sent ragged flashes of pain through his leg and a wetness there told him that it had begun to bleed anew, but he crawled doggedly on until at last he was in the shadow of the building, with the bulk of the structure between him and Pomeroy.

He lay quietly for a long minute, letting the pain subside. When he was once again ready to move, he lifted his head and saw the girl crouching in the shed's protection. Gathering his strength, he got to his feet and lunged the short distance to her side. She whirled at the sound and her hand flew to her mouth in a gesture of fear.

"Don't make a sound," Grimshaw whispered. "You all right?"

Melissa looked at him for a full, breathless moment, the fear and surprise still dulling her senses, and then all at once she gave way and was in his arms, sobbing out her terror. All the cool reserve was gone, all the fierce pride — and she was as any woman in a man's strong arms, feeling their protection.

"You all right?" Grimshaw asked again after the storm had passed.

The girl nodded. "It was terrible. They came and Pomeroy asked me to come outside so we could talk. I did, and then they set fire to the place. One of them held me, but I broke away and hid, and they've been hunting for me. I lay in the ditch and one of them passed me by so close I could almost touch him. I was trying to reach the river, where I could hide in the willows."

She stopped after the rush of words and flung a long glance at the flames. "Everything I own in the world is in there," she said.

Grimshaw turned to look. His leg buckled and a spasm of pain ran across his face.

"You're hurt," she said quickly, but he brushed her aside, his eyes on Caine Pomeroy and his riders, still moving about the yard of the burning house. A man galloped into the fan of light, and Grimshaw recognized Siddons as the latter pulled up alongside Pomeroy and spoke rapidly. Kingpin's owner sat perfectly still until Siddons was through, eyes fastened to the backs of his hands folded on the saddle horn. Then he raised his head.

"Find that girl!" he ordered, his voice carrying plainly. "When we get her, Grimshaw will come looking for us."

Grimshaw turned back to Melissa. "My horse is tied to that big juniper down near the draw," he said, reaching into his shirt pocket. "Get on him and double back to the willows and follow the river until you're away from here. Ride to town as fast as you can."

"Nobody will help . . . not against Pomeroy," she said.

Grimshaw shook his head. "I know. Here's some money. There's a train that goes through about daylight. Buy yourself a ticket and go home to your people."

He pressed the money into her hand, and for a time she was still. Kingpin's men were moving about more widely now, yelling back and forth, extending their circle of search.

"And you?" she said finally.

Grimshaw shook his head. "I'll be all right. The big thing is for you to get out of here as fast as possible."

Again Melissa seemed to consider, and Grimshaw, impatient at the delay, pressed her to movement. "Not much time. They'll comb this place to the inch. You'll have to hurry and, if anything happens . . . don't stop. Keep going."

She said then: "Good bye, Dan. I wish . . ."

There was a brief time when he felt her lips brush his own, and then she was gone, running toward the juniper.

Watching Kingpin narrowly, Grimshaw checked the gun he had taken from Siddons and finding it the same caliber as his own, replaced the spent cartridge in the cylinder. Glancing back once, he saw Melissa had reached the buckskin and was climbing into the saddle.

At the same moment a shout went up from one of the riders. Grimshaw turned to see the girl racing for the willows, and, bringing his gun up quickly, he laid a shot at the feet of Pomeroy's horse, checking the pursuit before it could get started.

"Don't move!" he called out.

A man swore and the plunging horses settled down after the echoes of the shot had drifted away. Dust and smoke lifted up into the night and Pomeroy's sardonic voice reached out and placed its aggravation on Grimshaw's nerves.

"Glad you're here. Saves us looking you up later, friend. Got a little matter to settle with you."

He stopped, apparently thinking Grimshaw would answer, but when an answer failed to come, he said: "Just sit easy, boys. The fire is dying down fast, and, when it does, there won't be much light. Plenty of time."

Grimshaw counted seven riders in view. One was missing, and he wondered if the man were elsewhere in the shadows, or just hidden by the last standing wall of the razed house. Cautiously then, keeping from sight of the men, he moved to the opposite side of the shed. The missing man was not in the yard, and Grimshaw realized that he was somewhere in the darkness, possibly circling around to get behind him or flank him while his attention was drawn to Pomeroy and the others.

The cold coolness was upon Grimshaw then, but this time he was also touched with a running excitement. His back to the shed, he replaced the cartridge he had fired and waited, listening for the slightest sound, the scrape of a man's clothing, the click of a boot as it clashed with stone. It didn't come, and in the rigid stillness his leg began to throb more intensely. The men on their horses, pinned down, squirmed in their saddles. The fire had dropped to a dozen small tongues flickering palely in the night, and back in the hills beyond the Shannin a coyote set up his complaint.

Tension built up until it was a great, oppressive thing, smothering the small clearing. Suddenly the last of the flames were out and there was only the star shine to break the dark solidness. Pomeroy and the others became indistinct shapes, vague shadows in the gloom. It was then he heard the man behind him.

Favoring his leg, he crouched and moved around the shed, reasoning that if he could no longer see Pomeroy and his men, they could not see him either. Keeping low, he crossed the short space between the shed and the ruined house and pressed himself against the still warm wall. Horses were moving about quietly and the creak of leather and muffled *tunk-tunk* of hoofs in the deep dust were the only sounds.

"Get off your horses . . ." — Pomeroy's voice broke out of the darkness — "he can't get far."

"We'll get him, Caine," Whitcomb's voice came from across the yard. "Don't worry."

Grimshaw, standing silently against the wall, heard the distinct scuff of boots near the tool shed and waited in the blackness for the man to appear, to cross over and come to him. He held his gun waist high and ready, but the man, finding no one at the shed, called out — "Not here!" — and moved out into the open. It was Ryan, and he passed within twenty feet of Grimshaw.

Grimshaw started to go back, working slowly, hearing the sounds of the others beating around the yard and the other buildings. A horse stumbled and a man cursed, and another voice said irritably: "Get that horse away from here." Grimshaw moved on stiffly, picking each step carefully, keeping close to the building but far enough away to prevent the scrape of his clothing against the charred wood. He was rapidly becoming the center of the circling men and he recognized the urgency of getting away from the building, off to one side, if possible.

He felt the corner of the structure and waited, warned by some inner instinct, before making the turn. For several long minutes he was motionless, flattened against the smoking timbers, and then quite suddenly Caine Pomeroy, coming from the opposite direction, was before him.

Sheer animal hatred tore at the man's face and his gun blossomed bright orange in his hand, but Grimshaw was already lurching to one side. He felt the breath of the bullet even as his own gun added its flat, quick echo. Pomeroy fell backward from the shock of the heavy slug, and sprawled half in, half out of the burned house.

"Here! Over here!" a man shouted.

Grimshaw, on his knees, crawled for the protection of the tool shed, ignoring the pain that screamed through his leg. Feet pounded across the yard, slowed, and men came up to the prostrate figure cautiously.

"It's Pomeroy!" a voice said, peculiar in its high, wondering pitch. "He's dead!"

"Dead?" The answer was an echo, unbelieving. The impossible had happened.

Silence ran on for a time, nobody saying anything, each man having his own thoughts.

"I'm blowing this country," Ryan's voice said then, and Grimshaw smiled, thinking of the seed he had planted. A man's mind was a funny thing. An acorn of doubt placed there flowers quickly into a full-blown tree.

Ryan turned to catch his horse. The others watched, and then they, too, were moving to their mounts and pounding out of the yard in a steady drum of hoofs. Only one man remained — Britt Whitcomb. He stood over Pomeroy's body and Grimshaw watched as he awkwardly removed his hat. His voice was choked, almost like a sobbing child.

"Don't you worry none, Caine. I'll square this for you. I'll take care of it."

Grimshaw knew then there was no future in that moment and, not being a man given to avoiding the consequences he had built up after the cards had fallen, he stepped out into the starlight. His own gun was in its holster as was Whitcomb's.

"Right here, Whitcomb," he said.

The foreman wrenched at his gun, fired briefly. Once again Grimshaw felt the wind of the lead and it threw his own aim wild. His bullet chunked into the wall behind the foreman. He fired the second time as Whitcomb brought his gun down from recoil. The man dropped, falling across Caine Pomeroy's legs.

Grimshaw staggered to the shed and leaned wearily against it. For a minute he was sick and the sharp odor of gunpowder was a mockery in his nostrils. Later, tired almost to insensibility by the strain and weakened by his own throbbing wound, he caught up one of the two horses, and, pulling himself into the saddle, started the long ride to town. The first rose streaks of dawn were just beginning to fan out from behind the eastern hills, and, as he topped the first rise, the lonely *hoot* of a train drifted through the quiet.

He pulled the horse to a stop, his thoughts having their strong way with him. That would be the train carrying Melissa away, taking her out of his life, taking her back to her home and people. The futility of his own life was heavy upon him then, and he felt worn and drawn and filled with a disgust for the uselessness of his ways. This could have been the country, the land, the valley, and she, he knew then, was the girl if only they both had recognized it. Now there was only the next hill and the one beyond and the one beyond that until one day there were no more and a man was through his riding.

He looked up, hearing the approach of a running horse. Quickly alert, he shifted his gun to a more convenient position and waited, following the sound as it came up the river. A horse and rider broke into view in the half light, and then Melissa was racing across the short distance toward him. Grimshaw swung stiffly from the saddle, leaning heavily against his horse, and, as she came to him, her face a mirror of her feelings, he took her into his arms.

"I couldn't go, Dan," she said. "I had to come back."

Grimshaw held her close to him, letting the pure song of it pour through his aching body, savoring every moment of it. He said then soberly: "You shouldn't have. I haven't anything to offer you except a long trail. I'm no sodbuster."

Melissa looked up at his face, eyes shining and bright. "Then we'll just ride on . . . but maybe someday we'll find the right place and stop."

Bitter Sunset

Again that day there was no break in the heat. The sun continued to pour down from the brilliant Arizona sky upon the small encampment of Mimbres Apache people clustered about their poor wickiups in the scant sage and mesquite growth on the floor of the cañon. They had followed their fierce old chief there, believing his words, and now many were dead and many more were dying, and it seemed the end for all of them was close.

It was not the lack of food that brought the Dark One, as they termed death, into their camp. Although the last pony had been slaughtered and eaten, there were still the animal hides stretched over poles forming the tent-like wickiups that could be taken down and boiled with herbs and roots by the squaws and converted into a sort of evil-smelling but nourishing soup. It was water they needed.

The rains had not come. The sinkholes and the springs were dry. The last of the Great Thirsts was upon them. Even their bones clamored for moisture. The strong were yet living, imploring Unsen to send them rain, but it seemed to the suffering Apaches that their chief god had deserted them in their hour of need.

Goyahkla was aware of all these things. He was a short, squat old man, typical of his race in build and appearance. He sat in the meager shade of his wickiup, the skin of his face hanging in loose, dry folds; sunken, hollow eyes squinted against the glare. His mouth was set in a cruel, gray line, twisted and expressive of his terrible hate. He showed no outward signs of his need, but inwardly his belly rolled and clenched spasmodically with its pain, while his mind struggled to find some explanation for the predicament he and his people were in.

It was hard to believe the gods had forsaken him, that they would allow him, the greatest and bravest of all the Apache chiefs, to be brought to such circumstances by the "god-damns", the white men — that name having been given to them by the Apache people because of the frequency with which they used the expression — and he could find no reason why he should be punished so cruelly. He had fought them all, fiercely, bravely, and bitterly, many times and often against tremendous, overwhelming odds, asking no favors. Now, why should such a fate befall him?

Yet there was one thought in the back of his dark, old mind that likely disturbed him greatly. It was always there and he could never avoid it, although he tried many times to veer away from it. That was the occasion, years ago, while he was still a young brave in the tribe of Mangas Coloradas — Red Sleeves, the god-damns called him — when he had scoffed at his chief's efforts to make peace with the white men. His youthful impatience, coupled with an inflexible hatred for those he knew invariably spoke with forked-tongues, made him wonder often at the wisdom of the Apache chieftain. And when that peace was never fully realized and Mangas Coloradas finally died attempting to obtain it, all doubts crystallized. There could be no peace with the white people and he was unwilling to accept the idea that the god-damns would have their way despite the Apaches.

That was when the Mimbres tribe, enraged and embittered, turned to him for leadership, and he had led them well. He had thrown havoc across the hills and mesas in swift, bloody retaliation and all trails became unsafe. He had proven himself a fearless warrior, knowing no measure of mercy or pity, and the numberless bodies bleaching under the sun were grim testimony to his ferocity. First the *nakai-yes*, the Mexicans from the south, had felt the fury of his onslaughts. And then the white-eyes, or the god-damns, with their long wagon trains, their mining camps where they dug the yellow iron *pesh-klitso*, the solitary trappers and traders — all feared him and the ruthlessness of his cunning mind. Even the yellow-legs, the soldiers with their long knives, knew what terror meant.

But something was wrong, he knew. All such things had been accomplished and yet here were he and his people, reduced to helpless, suffering shadows and the powerful, feared Apache nation was the victim of its own gods. He licked his dry lips, considering the question that had faced him before: had Mangas Coloradas been right? Had Cochise been right? Was

there no stopping the god-damns and the *nakai-yes* —
no driving them from the country of the Mimbres
people? Once he had been sure. Once he had scorned
such thoughts, but now there was a doubt.

He remembered now. He remembered the time
when he and many of the warriors had accompanied
Mangas Coloradas far into the Chiricahua Mountains
where Cochise had summoned them for council. It had
been cold and disagreeable. He had missed the
warmness of the sun. He had wanted to leave the dark
cañons and return to the mesas and low hills long
before the meeting was over. But it was an important
gathering; the presence of many medicine men,
shamans, had indicated this, and with the others he had
remained there, letting Cochise have his say.

The chief had spoken first of the war with the
nakai-yes. He had told how the Apache people had
been able to hold their own against those invaders from
the south. Gradually he had worked up to the coming
of the god-damns.

Goyahkla had not listened to the wisdom in the
words but rather had sought reasons against Cochise's
statements. He had watched and listened from the folds
of his blanket in stony silence, his mind accepting none
of the truths.

"Our lands have been overrun by the white men,"
Cochise had said. "Their ways are many and confusing
and there is no understanding of them, but there can be
peace . . . there must be peace. Even though they tell us
they are our friends and then turn upon us and betray
us. There is no rest for us. They hunt us like we hunt

the wild animals. As we get better weapons, they get still better ones. Although we kill many, they kill even more of us, and we grow fewer while the white men grow as the blades of grass on the hillsides."

Cochise had paused, his sharp eyes seeking out the faces of the warriors circled about the fire. Then he had gone on: "Since long before our times, the bravery and wisdom of our people has been a known thing. We have always fought for the things we thought ours, but the time has now come when we must consider gravely even that . . . for by war, we have gained nothing. We have lost much. It would be better to have peace with the white men, to try and understand them and their ways, for soon there will be no Apache race and all will be finished."

The deep and profound silence that had fallen upon the council was proof of the surprise Cochise had given them. Then, slowly, one by one, they had stated their own opinions. Some had agreed. Others had not. And those in the latter group had taken their leave, refusing to consider longer such a cowardly procedure. Among those had been Goyahkla.

Looking about his present *campo del muerto*, camp of death, Goyahkla had reason to wonder, for Mangas Coloradas had gone ahead with his plan and made his peace, and now, although he was dead and those who had followed him were living upon a reservation, fenced in like cattle, they had prospered. Here was defeat, a bitter medicine for Goyahkla. His dwindling forces had met and been routed by superior numbers of the blue-clad Long Knives. They lay now in the short hills, hiding like frightened coyotes, while a messenger, Coleto Negro, the last of his scouts, sought information as to the strength and the condition of the soldiers.

Goyahkla glanced to the sky again. If there could come rain, only a very little, then perhaps his warriors would take heart and recover courage and he could once more lead them against the Long Knives. But there was no promise of rain from that clear, brilliant blue overhead.

The sun dropped toward the west. Soon Coleto Negro would return. His mission had been one of dual purpose: to size up the enemy camp and deliver a message to the *nantan*, the commanding officer of the Long Knives, requesting that he return to the Apache wickiups with him. There was treachery in the plan for it was Goyahkla's intention to hold the *nan-tan* as prisoner if the soldiers fared as badly as the Mimbres people and force an armistice that would allow the Apaches to escape. If the Long Knives did not fare as the Apaches — that would be something else, and Goyahkla refused to consider what then would be his actions. At that moment would come the time to decide.

He listened for any sounds that would announce the return of Coleto Negro, but there was nothing save the low moaning of his people and the dry clack of insects. He wondered if Coleto Negro had failed, if his weakened condition had prevented him from reaching the Long Knife camp. This he quickly dismissed as not possible. The scout would get through. If he did not return, it would be because of the treachery of the white men. Thinking of such, the old chief went into a seething rage. That he was considering the same sort of treachery, once the *nan-tan* of the soldiers was in his camp, was a different matter . . .

Not far away, Lieutenant Gatewood (some say his given name was Jerome, others Charles) followed closely upon the heels of the Apache, Coleto Negro. His guide was in a weakened condition. Several times the Indian faltered and stumbled. But they pressed on in the afternoon's fading light. He was old to the ways of the Apache people, this young soldier, and had spent many years among them. Some were his friends, others respected him, but he had no illusions about them. He moved along, ever wary of a trap. But it was worth the risk, he felt, and he had sent word back to his commanding officer, Captain Lawton, as to his plans.

He carried his pistol in his hand, ready, for not again would he be caught napping as he had been once before and now sported a long scar down his left thigh as evidence. The Apaches were hard to figure, always doing the unexpected, and for such he was alert and unceasingly on guard. He fell to pondering the message the scout had brought — a message that stated Goyahkla and his people were without food and water and that the chief would talk of peace. But far back in Gatewood's mind a bell rang, warning him that all was not so simple as it might seem. It appeared to him to be small reason for surrender. Never before had such minor things as food and water been cause for an Apache capitulation. At such periods they were like

111

wounded grizzlies, back to the wall, at bay and thoroughly dangerous. But after considering, he deemed the risk worth the try and, after all, that was his business, as it was the duty of all soldiers in the U.S. 6th Cavalry to do all possible in bringing about the end of the Indian trouble.

Undoubtedly he had his moments of indecision, for he was a brave and intelligent man, and he knew he was dealing with one of the wiliest and most ruthless of all the Apaches, this Goyahkla. Perhaps he was moving straight to his death and that thought rankled him for it was no way to die. In battle, yes, but not in a trap into which he had walked of his own volition. A man taking up a rifle for the Army naturally assumed his chances, and, while death was thereafter a never too-distant partner and every man eventually came face to face with eternity, this being bait in the hands of the Apaches carried little appeal. But it was not over yet — and there was that chance that it was all in good faith.

Ahead he noticed the scout straighten a bit and seemingly take into himself added strength. At once he became alert, watching for some sort of surprise or treachery. None came. They rounded a heavy clump of brush and broke into a small clearing. The soldier checked abruptly, seeing the cluster of wickiups before him. At first glance the camp seemed deserted, but as his eyes probed into the shadows he made out the crouched and prone figures. Looking swiftly around, he realized he was standing almost in the center of a ring of Apache braves.

112

Long versed in the ways of such people, knowing the workings of their minds, the soldier throttled the fear and surprise that sprang into his throat. He strode slowly toward the hunched form of the man he knew to be Goyahkla. The scout had deserted him and stood now behind his chief.

Gatewood lifted his head, palm outward in the sign of peace, and faced the old warrior. "My brother called for me. I am here," he said.

"Who are you who speaks my tongue?" Goyahkla demanded. He knew full well the identity of Gatewood but such was his way. "I sent word I would speak with the *nan-tan*. You are not the *nan-tan*."

"I am a little *nan-tan*. I come because my white brother speaks not your language. I talk for him."

The chief shrugged and shifted his position, his rifle coming to point straight at the soldier's belly. He studied Gatewood's face for any change of expression, any indication of fear, but there was none.

"It is well. But why are you not afraid? No white man has before entered the camp of Goyahkla and lived to speak of it. Do you not fear?"

"You gave your word that the white *nan-tan* could come and go in peace. I trust the word of the chief Goyahkla."

The Apache snorted. "What knows the white men of honor? Many times have they given their word, only to break it. The memory of their treachery is great in my mind."

That moment was critical and Gatewood knew it. Much rested upon his reply, and he thought carefully

113

for words. He waited until the low muttering about the camp subsided, then spoke, making his voice loud and distinct. "There are among the white people as there are among the Apaches those who speak with the forked tongue. There are those who do not wish the Apache people and the white people to be at peace and forever will they make trouble. Do not blame us for the faults of the few. Believe those of us who would be your friends."

Suddenly there was a commotion behind the chief. A warrior, who had been standing, fell forward, clutching his throat. The man struck against a nearby wickiup and slid quietly to the ground, his mouth and eyes going wide. Back in the darkness a squaw began to wail in a high, quavering voice. Goyahkla paused momentarily, seeming to listen. Afterward, he tossed a handful of branches upon the fire and watched it flare up.

"Why do not the Long Knives attack and kill us?" he asked. "We are weak and starving. Now is the time. Were the Apache warriors in such position as your soldiers, they would show no mercy. Do the Long Knives have women's hearts?"

"It is not our wish to kill you and your people, my brother, although to do so would be easy now. As the bear might kill the rabbit. But we are not a cruel people nor are we weak. A man can be strong and brave and not be cruel."

Goyahkla shook his head, having no understanding for it. There was no such word, no such emotion, as pity in the Apache make-up; he played the game of war for keeps, no holds barred, no quarter asked or given.

Pity was but an indication of weakness. He said: "You would make us prisoners. You would take us from our land and fence us in and we would die."

"You are dying now, my brother," Gatewood replied. "Already, while you and your people starve, other Apaches on the reservation grow old with full bellies and are happy."

"Not truth!" the chief exclaimed. "There is no happiness when one lives like cattle! Give me your promise that we can return to our land and there will be peace."

"I can give you no such promise. You must trust the big *nan-tan* Miles. He is truthful and fair and will treat you kindly."

"We will not become as cattle!" Goyahkla shrilled again, drawing himself erect. "Such is for the weak and for the squaws. My warriors are fierce and brave!"

Gatewood's reply was low but clear and it reached out and touched every corner of the camp. "Bravery alone cannot feed hungry mouths, my brother."

At his words the old chief seemed to crumple. His shoulders sagged and he stared into the fire for a long minute. His thoughts must have ranged back over the years, over the many wars and battles he had fought and the terrible destruction he had thrown across the hills and mesas — all for nothing. He lifted his eyes toward *Holos*, the sun who had been his friend but like all others had forsaken him now and was dropping beyond the rims of hills in the west. It was sunset, a bitter sunset.

"*Enju*," he murmured, "it is finished." He got slowly and heavily on his feet, bringing the rifle into the crook of his arm. "It is finished. We shall go to the big *nan-tan*, but the Apaches shall not go as dogs. We shall keep our weapons, for we are proud. Let us go."

Lieutenant Gatewood, be it Charles or Jerome, of the United States 6th Cavalry, looked at the fallen chief and a wave of pity passed through him for this once powerful old warrior. He had been a brave and worthy enemy and he had fought fiercely under the only code he knew, be it ever so opposed and distasteful to the white man's way of thinking. And now it was all over. But he stood there, firelight flickering upon his dark features, defiance still in his black eyes, proud even in defeat.

The impact of that moment was upon Gatewood. The long, frightful campaign was over. The fact's tremendous importance raced through him like a grass fire. The chief the Indians called Goyahkla had surrendered, Goyahkla, the terror of the Southwest, the scourge of both the Americans and the Mexicans, who knew him as Gerónimo.

116

A Question of Faith

It was the time of war, the bloody, senseless conflict of ideologies now mercifully reeling toward its finish. New Mexico, having had its brief fling with shot and shell, hung suspended in a neglected vacuum aware of the struggle only by reports from far distant battlefields or the occasional glimpse of a blue-uniformed patrol riding a remote trail.

Mid-July and the afternoon heat lay across the broad plains and choppy hills in a blistering haze. Overhead the sky was cobalt steel, and along its edges cloud mountains piled up in masses of jumbled cotton batting to rim a breathlessly hot world in which nothing moved but vagrant dust devils and the stagecoach bound for Rinconada.

Driver Luke Colegrove, the leather ribbons laced between his fingers sawing his arms back and forth as the double span of lathered blacks pressed against the harness, flung a sideward glance to Ed Drummond, that day beside him on the box.

"Anything?"

Drummond again swept the savage terrain with his keen scrutiny. He shook his head, mopped at the sweat oozing freely from his weathered face. "Nope . . .

117

nothin'.'" He waited a minute as the coach slowed around a curve, rocked precariously, righted itself, and plunged on. "You figure Cannon knowed what he was talkin' about? Never heard of Quantrill's bunch this far west before."

Colegrove, an acid little man with hawk-like features and a straggling yellow mustache, said: "He knowed. Them guerrillas been stopping coaches all over the country, hunting them two women."

Drummond digested that in silence. Then: "Figure to tell the passengers? Bound to throw a powerful scare into them."

"They got a right to know. We get to Cook's, I'll speak my piece. You do some talking to that hostler. See if he's seen any signs of them. Was ten, maybe twelve in the bunch. Cannon wasn't sure."

Thirty minutes later they rushed into Cook's Station, rolling the dust ahead of them in a great, yellow boil, and came to a sliding stop. The hostler trotted up with fresh horses and immediately began to make his change. Drummond, not relinquishing his rifle, turned to him. Luke Colegrove swung down, yanked open the coach door.

"Ten minutes, folks. Stretch your legs and get yourself a swallow of water." He wheeled away, entered the low-roofed adobe hut where further refreshments were to be had.

The passengers began to crawl stiffly from the cramped confines of the stage into the glaring sunlight. First, a plump, gray woman, middle-aged and the wife of a territorial delegate. Next came her daughter, just

turned seventeen. She was pretty, blue-eyed, and filling
out her stylishly cut traveling suit to perfection. On
their way to visit relatives in Silver City, it was said.
Third fare was a portly cattleman from Las Vegas,
Armstrong by name; he was prone to much dozing and,
when awake, fiddled constantly with a gold toothpick
attached to a thin chain issuing from the top
buttonhole of his checked vest. He was a man who
moved deliberately and with care, his ponderous bulk
pressing the springs of the coach to basic level as he
shifted to one side and emerged through the door. The
fourth was Dave Kirby. Young, barely in his twenties in
fact, with a rashness upon his features, a caged wildness
glowing in his eyes. Handcuffs linked his wrists, and
these glinted as sunlight touched the nickeled metal.
His journey would end at Rinconada where he would
stand trial for murder. He halted, leaned against the
rear wheel of the vehicle in studied insolence as he
awaited the tall lawman who followed close on his
heels. He was John Prince, marshal of Springville, in
the process of delivering a prisoner. Lean of face, lank
of body, a heavy personal trouble now lay upon him like
a shroud, turning him taciturn and cold, and, when he
placed his narrow glance on Dave Kirby, fresh anger
stirred within him for he knew the outlaw was aware of
that trouble.

Kirby had been present during that hour before the
stage departed Springville. He had witnessed the
stormy scene, heard the bitter words that had passed
between the tall lawman and his wife, Kate, Jealousy in

119

a man is a pitiless scourge, forcing the worst to the surface — and the soul of John Prince had been laid bare before the outlaw.

Armstrong paused, stretched, yawned. The two women looked about uncertainly. Kirby caught the eye of the younger, smiled, his expression suddenly boyish.

"Water's inside, ma'am," he said, and nodded at the hut.

The girl thanked him and, with her mother, moved toward the sagging structure. At that moment Colegrove appeared, wiping at his mouth with the back of a hand. He glanced at Drummond, still in conversation with the hostler, halted, brushed his sweat-stained hat to the back of his head.

John Prince swore softly under his breath. He'd hoped to deliver Kirby and return quickly to Springville. The thought of Kate alone — with time on her hands — with Wilson Coyle subtly pressing his flattery and attentions upon her gouged into him like a saw-edged blade. He had not wanted to make the trip to Rinconada in the first place, but there'd been no choice. Now it appeared something was coming up that would keep him away even longer.

Resentment sharpened his tone. "Now, why . . . ?"

"Guerrillas." Colegrove spat. "Part of Quantrill's bunch. Been stopping stages on this road last few days."

"Quantrill?" Armstrong echoed in frank disbelief. "This far west?"

The old driver shrugged. "Been spotted east of here. And in Texas. Just about everywhere, in fact."

There was a lengthy silence in the streaming sunlight broken only by the rattle of harness metal as the hostler worked at his chore.

John Prince said: "You carrying a money shipment?"

Colegrove wagged his head. "Only a smidgin of mail."

"Then why," Mrs. Russell said, dabbing at the patches of sweat on her face with a lace handkerchief, "would they want to bother us?"

Colegrove looked directly at the woman, his beaten features solemn. "Reckon it's you they're wanting, ma'am. You and your daughter."

Mrs. Russell caught at her breath. The handkerchief went to her lips to stifle a cry. Instantly Martha placed her arm around the older woman's shoulders. She stared at Colegrove.

"Why . . . why us?"

"Your daddy's a big man in this here country. Was I guessing, I'd say they figured to hold you for ransom."

"Maybe," Armstrong said. "Heard tell how Quantrill's bunch is always pulling raids to get women for . . ."

"Forget it," Prince snapped. He swung his angry, impatient attention to the stagecoach driver. "Why the hell didn't you say something about this back at the fort? Could've asked for a cavalry escort."

Colegrove spat into the dust. "Didn't know about it. Just got the word at the last stop. Anyway," he added, glancing over the party, "I expect there's enough of us to give them an argument, if they try stopping us."

Prince allowed his jaundiced gaze to travel over the group. Enough — hell! Two women, an outlaw a man

121

couldn't trust beyond arm's length, and a fat cow-nurse who'd likely curl up on the floor at the first shot. Only Drummond, the shotgun rider, might be relied upon for help — and, if the raiders were smart, they'd shoot him off the box at the start. Far as Colegrove was concerned, he could be counted out of it; he'd have his hands full with the team.

Mrs. Russell began to weep raggedly. Martha drew her closer, patting her on the arm gently.

Colegrove bit off a fresh chew of tobacco. "Right sorry I had to tell you all this, but I figured you ought to know. Now, everybody get aboard. Let's get moving."

Drummond came up at that point. "Pete says he ain't seen nobody around that maybe looks like guerrillas. Says he seen smoke west of here this mornin'."

Colegrove thought for a moment. "Could've been pilgrims . . . Or maybe 'Paches," he added as he started for the coach.

Armstrong hurried into the hut for his drink. The women turned, Mrs. Russell supported by her daughter. Dave Kirby stepped up quickly to assist, handing as best he could in handcuffs first the older woman, and then Martha into the heat-trapped interior of the vehicle. Prince saw the girl touch the outlaw with her glance, expressing her thanks. The thought — *Why will a woman always go for his kind?* — passed through his mind. Shrugging then, he followed Kirby into the coach, settled himself on the forward seat next to the outlaw. A moment later Armstrong, puffing from the short sprint, took his place on the rear bench.

Colegrove shouted to the team, and they lunged forward, yanking the stage into forward motion with a violent rocking. Dust at once lifted between the opposed seats, began to rise and fall in a powdery cloud as the heat-charged air surged through the enclosure. In the road's deep ruts the coach crackled and popped and groaned from stress, those sounds blending gradually with Luke Colegrove's strident shouting.

Talk, desultory at best prior to the halt at Cook's Station, was now a dead issue, each passenger wrapped deeply in his own thoughts. John Prince was thinking of the past, of the seven years of married life with Kate who had grown more beautiful as time went by. Once he had been proud of her beauty, was vaguely complimented that she was the target for other men's eyes. Now it was a red-hot iron searing through his chest. How had that come to be? When had it begun?

Somewhere, sometime . . . One day Kate and he were as any married couple, happy, content insofar as means permitted, loving in a comfortable, satisfying way, and then the next there had been change. Their status had not altered, yet there was a difference between them, a sullen anger, a wariness and suspicion that fattened on the hours while they were apart.

Wilson Coyle, that old friend of bygone years, had much to do with it, he was sure. Not that he knew anything of certainty; it was simply — well, the way things looked, sounded. And in his profession he had learned to have little faith in mankind, and always to expect the worst.

The heat increased. Armstrong removed his coat and hung it across the window sill, unbuttoned his straining vest. Mrs. Russell improvised a fan with her purse, waved persistently at her flushed face. She had recovered her composure, no longer wept but sat now perfectly quiet, her pale features frozen. Beside her Martha studied her fingertips, eyes downcast, dark lashes resting upon her cheeks. Once she looked up, placed her attention on John Prince.

"Will we get help at the next stop?"

"Not this side of Silver City," he snapped, the sharpness of his voice betraying the turmoil raging within him.

The girl colored, glanced away, chastened by his abruptness.

"Don't you mind the marshal none, ma'am," Kirby said in a light, mocking tone. "He plain don't like nobody. Not even hisself."

Prince shifted his bitter glance to the outlaw but there was no change in his expression. He shrugged as the coach slammed on down the rutted road. Let the bastard talk, let him run off at the mouth, his days were numbered. As far as he personally was concerned, it didn't matter what others thought. The whole human race could go to hell.

The shouts of Luke Colegrove lifted and the coach began to pitch and sway with greater intensity. Armstrong thrust his head through the window, made his absent survey, and murmured — "Coming into the hills." — and settled back. Prince glanced through the opening, saw the flat country swelling gradually into definite knolls that grew larger in the distance.

Outside the hard running of the horses was a steady drumming. The iron tires of the wheels screamed through the loose sand, clanged against rock, and the dust was an enveloping cloud racing the coach. Luke's yells had become a constant sound lashing at the horses at they began to climb a long grade. Frowning, red buttes closed in on either side and suddenly they were in a narrow channel.

Good place for an ambush, John Prince thought, and that induced him to sweep back the skirt of his coat, make his pistol more easily available. Martha Russell noted that and laid her questioning glance upon him. He merely shook his head, turned away.

The coach began to slow up as the drag of the grade took its toll of the horse's speed. Colegrove's yells increased, well interspaced with profanity, but they were drawing near a crest as the diminishing height of the buttes indicated.

Suddenly they were on the summit, wheeling around a sharp bend and picking up speed. Unexpectedly they began to slow. Ed Drummond shouted something unintelligible. Immediately following there came the sharp, spiteful *crack* of his rifle. Prince stiffened, drew his weapon, and twisted about to peer through the window. A dozen yards or so ahead a scatter of riders milled about on the road, were blocking their passage.

"I'm going through 'em!" Luke Colegrove yelled, and began to ply the whip. "Hang on!"

125

Prince threw a quick glance to Armstrong, was surprised to see the big man draw his long-barreled pistol, rest it upon the window sill. He looked then to the girl.

"Down on the floor . . . quick!"

She obeyed instantly. The lawman motioned Kirby to her vacated seat. The outlaw complied hastily, and, when it was done, the girl was below them, protected by their legs while Mrs. Russell was sandwiched securely between Armstrong on one side, and Dave Kirby on the other. Prince thus had the rear seat to himself, enabling him to slide back and forth and watch both sides of the road.

Ed Drummond's rifle cracked again, and then became a continuing hammering as answering shots came from the road. The coach began to sway and reel and dust became a choking, oppressive factor in breathing. Prince cast a calculating look at Mrs. Russell. She would be breaking down, going to pieces any moment now, and they'd have more problems. He'd order Kirby to look after her, keep her out of the way.

Reaching inside his coat, he drew a second pistol, the one he'd taken off Dave Kirby and now evidence in the pending case, laid it on the seat. From a pocket he obtained a bandanna into which a handful of spare cartridges had been placed, dropped them beside Kirby's gun.

"Could give you a hand," the outlaw said, ducking his head at the weapon.

Prince shrugged. "No, thanks."

126

"My neck, too," Kirby said.

"But my responsibility," the lawman replied, and closed the subject.

Drummond's firing continued, and now Armstrong began to lay down his shots as they drew abreast the raiders. The acrid smell of powder smoke at once filled the coach, overriding the dust, and Colegrove's shouts began to mingle with others coming from the road. Bullets began to *thud* into the coach, dimpling the paneling. Armstrong jumped when one splintered the wood above his head.

They reeled through the cluster of waiting riders, two of which were falling slowly from their saddles. A dark-whiskered man wearing a faded forage cap swerved in close, mouth open in a wild yell. Prince took deliberate aim, pressed off his shot. The man jolted, wilted, fell. Ed Drummond's rifle had gone silent, and, wondering about it, the lawman looked back. The guard was a crumpled bundle of dusty clothing in the road.

Prince swore silently. Armstrong and him. That was it now. Another guerrilla hove into view alongside, lips curled into a grin as he aimed a bullet at the rancher. Prince fired at point-blank range. The raider threw up his arms, slid from his running horse.

Armstrong triggered his weapon with cool regularity, pausing only to reload. Prince guessed he'd figured him wrong. Mrs. Russell, too. She was a huddled, silent shape between the cattleman and Kirby. He glanced at the girl. Her face had paled, but when she saw him looking, she smiled faintly.

Shots from the guerrillas had slackened. They were behind the coach now, on the road, regrouping. Colegrove's unexpected decision to barrel straight through them had caught them unawares, thrown them off balance. And it would be for only a few moments; already they were beginning to give chase.

Prince made a hasty calculation. Still a dozen or more in the raiding party. He and Armstrong could not hope to hold them off for long. He thrust his head through the window, looked beyond the wildly running team. A distance to the right he saw a low structure standing near the road.

"That place . . . ?" he yelled at Colegrove. "What is it?"

"Baker's Ranch. Deserted . . . not much . . ."

"Pull in!" the lawman shouted above the hammering of the horses. "Fort up . . . our only chance!"

Colegrove bobbed his head in agreement. The team was running free on the downgrade and brake blocks now began to whine, go silent, whine again as the old driver alternately applied and released them to control the swaying vehicle.

Back on the seat Prince faced the others. "We're pulling off, going to hole up in an old ranch house. Be ready to jump and run for it when I give the word."

He waited for reaction — some pointless protest from Mrs. Russell, a complaint from Armstrong, a note of despair from the girl. None came. Dave Kirby lifted his chained wrists.

"Take them off, Marshal . . . and give me my gun. I'll help."

128

Prince grunted. "Forget it. All you need do is run for the door of that house when I tell you."

He threw his glance back down the road. In the dust-filled distance he could see the dim outlines of the raiders pounding in pursuit. They were nearer than he expected. Abruptly the coach was rocking dangerously, and the brakes were a constant screaming as they wheeled from the main ruts. The vehicle skidded, tipped on two wheels, and for a breathless instant John Prince thought they would overturn, but the coach righted itself and plunged on.

"Get ready!"

Prince shouted his warning above the crackling of the wood, protesting the savage treatment. He looked through the window. The ranch house was just ahead. He turned then to the road. The guerrillas were curving in toward them, beginning to shoot again. Colegrove yelled something and the coach began to slide, skid in close to the building.

"Now!" Prince cried and, flinging the door open, leaped out. He dropped to one knee, began to fire at the oncoming horsemen, conscious of the other passengers streaming by him. Above, on the box, Colegrove had taken up Drummond's rifle, was giving him aid. He looked over his shoulder. The two women and Armstrong were already inside the adobe-walled hut. Kirby was standing in the doorway. At once the lawman began to back toward the structure, shooting steadily with both pistols at the raiders.

"Colegrove!" he yelled. "Come on . . . inside!"

129

Lead slugs were thudding into the thick wall behind him, into the wood of the coach, kicking up dust around his feet.

"Colegrove!" he shouted again.

He gained the doorway, saw then that Colegrove could not hear. The driver lay half off the coach seat, head hanging, a broad circle of red staining his shirt front. Prince took a long step. He felt the solid smash of a bullet as it drove into his thigh. It spun him around. Instantly he felt Kirby's hands grab him into the shadowy interior of the house. Angered, he shook off the outlaw, booted the door shut, and dropped the bar into place. In that identical instant he heard the pound of hoofs and a surge of yells as the riders thundered into the yard. It had been close.

He wheeled, ignoring pain, knowing exactly what must be done — the other door barricaded, the wooden shutters closed and secured. Surprise ran through him when he saw that Armstrong and the women had already performed those vital chores, and there was for John Prince a brief moment of wonder at his bitter judgment of his fellow passengers.

"You've been hit!" Mrs. Russell exclaimed, hurrying toward him.

"Nothing serious," the lawman snapped, and moved to one of the front windows. He peered through a crack. "They'll be rushing us, but it won't be long till dark. If we can hold them off that long, like as not they'll give up and wait for morning."

Armstrong said — "Right." — in a business-like way. "I'll take the other door."

130

The house, a squat, one-room affair, evidently had been built for just such a critical moment except the owner would have had Indian attacks in mind. At each of the two doors and windows were small, round ports, blocked now by bags filled with sand. Prince pulled the bags away, looked again into the yard. The guerrillas had withdrawn fifty yards or so. They were in the process of bringing up a log they'd obtained from one of the decaying corrals.

"Armstrong!" Prince called without turning. "They're aiming to ram the door, break it in. Get up here and cover this other port."

The cattleman crossed the room quickly, stationed himself at the small opening.

There was a sudden flurry of covering gunshots, the sound of bullets driving into the adobe bricks. A chorus of wild yells lifted, and then a half a dozen men, supporting the log between them, rushed for the door.

Cool, Prince said: "Take the lead man on the right. I'll handle the left. Don't miss."

He waited until the guerrillas were not more than ten paces away, fired. His target was a squat, dark-faced man wearing an ill-assorted uniform of both Armies. The raider halted abruptly, fell. A step behind him the one singled out by Armstrong, hands clawing at his chest, was sinking to the ground. The remaining men, stalled by surprise, dropped the log and fled, evidently having overlooked the ports. Prince felled a third as they turned tail.

He was aware then of Mrs. Russell kneeling at his side. She had a strip of white cloth, probably ripped from her petticoat, draped across her shoulder and a knife in her hand. Deftly she slit the leg of his trousers.

"Never mind," he said, and tried to move away.

"Stand still," she replied sternly. "You're losing too much blood."

He looked down at her. Kate was like that, a little bossy when need be and it mattered to her. Armstrong's voice caught his attention.

"Stopped 'em cold. Fact is, couple of them are pulling out."

Prince glanced through his port. "Going for the rest of their bunch, I suspect. Seems we're going to be encircled. Means they aim to pin us down for the night."

"Be dark soon," Armstrong commented.

Mrs. Russell, her job completed, stepped back. Prince shifted his weight to the injured member. It was paining considerably now, and getting stiff. It would be giving him hell later.

The acrid smoke was clearing from the room. Martha Russell turned to the cattleman. "When the stage doesn't arrive at the next station, will they send somebody to find out why?"

"Hard to say," the cattleman answered. "Only one stop between here and Silver City, and that's a team change. This run's a bit irregular. Not apt to start thinking about it until noon, maybe even later."

Prince was fingering the ammunition in the bandanna. He glanced at Armstrong. "How many bullets you got?"

There was a moment of silence. Then: "Four rounds. You?"

"Dozen or so . . . Don't think we can depend on that bunch out there not making another try before morning. Best we stand watch at all four sides." He pivoted awkwardly, forgetting momentarily his injured leg, to face Mrs. Russell. "You shoot a pistol?"

"A little . . . I'm not sure."

From the depths of their murky quarters Dave Kirby spoke up. "Better give me that gun, Marshal."

"We'll get along without your help," the lawman answered.

"I don't know about that," Armstrong broke in doubtfully. "Ought to have a man, good with a gun, helping . . ."

"No prisoner of mine gets his hands on a weapon," Prince stated flatly. "I'll accept no help from one, either."

Mrs. Russell sighed audibly. "You're a foolish man. And one who's never learned the meaning of trust . . . or faith."

"You're figuring him right, ma'am," Kirby said, a thread of amusement in his voice. "He don't believe in nobody but himself . . . not even his own wife."

John Prince stiffened in the darkness. "That way a man never gets hurt," he said. "How about taking your stations?"

The minutes wore on, dragged into an hour, and night's chill settled over the room. Outside half a dozen small fires marked the positions of the raiders ringing the structure. Prince thought of Kate, wondered what she was doing at that moment. Immediately that sharp uneasiness began to gnaw at him. Was she with Wilson Coyle? Maybe with some other man he wasn't even aware of? And another thought reached him. Perhaps it would all end here. Perhaps the raiders would settle the whole problem for him — for her.

"Got any ideas what you'll be doing come the morning?" Dave Kirby asked, breaking the hush. "You got maybe fifteen bullets, Marshal. How long you figure you can stand off that bunch?"

"Long enough."

"For what? They hit us from all four sides at once and the ball will be over . . . for sure if they've got help coming."

Armstrong's voice showed interest. "You got something in mind?"

Kirby said: "Was I to get out of here and find me a horse, I could leg it for the next station, stir up a posse . . . maybe soldiers, even. They'd be here by sunrise."

"Could at that," Armstrong said. "Where'd you get a horse? Them raiders won't . . ."

"Take one of the coach team. Still standing out there in front. What do you say, Marshal? Don't care nothing about myself, or you, either, for that matter, but I sure hate to think of what'll happen to these ladies."

Prince sagged against the wall, took the weight off his injured leg. "You'd try anything to keep from facing that judge in Rinconada," he said in a dry, sarcastic voice. "Well, you're not fooling me. Once you went through that door, you'd line out straight for Mexico."

"Figured you'd be thinking about that," the outlaw said. "Only you're plumb wrong. I can make it past them ridge runners out there. You got my word I'll be waiting at the station for you."

Prince snorted. "Your word! Forget it, mister. I wouldn't trust you . . ." He stopped, feeling the hard circle of a gun's muzzle pressing into his ribs.

"I'm sorry," Mrs. Russell's voice, calm and confident, reached him. "I believe him. Make no mistake," she added quickly and prodded harder with the weapon as the lawman stirred. "I know enough about this weapon to pull the trigger . . . and this close I couldn't miss! At this moment I'm a desperate woman . . . a mother, and I'll do anything to keep my daughter from falling into the hands of those . . . those beasts out there. If Mister Kirby is willing to risk his life for us, I say we let him do so."

"You're a fool," Prince said in deep disgust. "He won't go for help. He's not interested in anything except a chance to get where the law can't touch him."

"I don't think so," the woman replied firmly. "Maybe it's your profession that's turned you hard . . . hard and bitter . . . and made you forget that there's usually some good in the worst of us."

"Usually, but not in this case," Prince said dryly. "Armstrong?"

"I agree with the lady," the cattleman said. "Our only chance."

"You saying you believe he'll do what he claims?"

"I'm willing to gamble on it. Comes a time, Marshal, when you've got to trust somebody. Man can't go

135

forever depending on himself. It's a question of having faith."

"Faith!" John Prince echoed scornfully, his thoughts, oddly, swinging to Kate. There was no value in faith, no substance — just as there was none in trust. Believe in either and a man found only heartbreak and disillusionment. Had he not learned that the hard way? Perhaps he had no real proof concerning Kate, but the signs were all there — at least what he considered indications. And true, she had denied them all, reproved him for his suspicions. But a man was a fool to ignore common logic.

"Just you stand easy," Armstrong's voice bored into his consciousness. "I'll be getting the keys for them handcuffs."

John Prince offered no resistance. He stood aside, watched them release Kirby, saw Mrs. Russell pass her gun to him, heard Armstrong murmur — "Good luck, boy." — and then his prisoner was slipping through the door opened only slightly. A heavy sigh escaped him. That was it. The end of it. He'd lost all — all.

The long night finally was over. The first flare of light began to spread across the plains and the shadows took on form. The two women, pale and worn from their vigilance, turned from the window ports. Armstrong forsook the rear door, noting that the encirclement had been withdrawn from around the shack. He stooped, peered through one of the front openings.

"About twice as many of them out there now," he said wearily. "Seems they've rousted out the head man."

Leg paining him intensely, Prince turned, glanced through his port. A lean individual in a gray Confederate Army uniform was in the center of the guerrilla party. He appeared to be outlining a plan to his followers.

"Looks like the boy got away," Armstrong commented. "Lead team horse is gone and there ain't no bodies except them three we cut down yesterday laying out there."

"He made it," Prince said. "Has that kind of luck. Right now I'd say he was halfway to the border." He paused, squinted into the glare. "Get yourself set. They're going to hit us. Don't waste no lead. We've only got . . ."

His words broke off. Faintly, riding the cold, clear air of the early morning, the notes of a bugle carried to him. Prince, disbelief covering his face, turned to Armstrong, then to Mrs. Russell — to the girl. The thrilling sound grew louder, closer. Abruptly guns began to crackle.

There was a quick rush of pounding hoofs, and through the port Prince saw a line of blue-clad riders, some with sabers flashing, sweep into the yard. More gunfire crashed. Two of the cavalrymen spilled from their horses, a half dozen guerrillas went down, others raced for their mounts. The line of blue swerved, gave chase.

"He did it!" Armstrong yelled happily, struggling with the bar that locked the door. "By heaven, the boy did it!"

John Prince shook his head. "Doubt that. Expect those soldiers were just riding by . . . happened to spot . . ."

But the others were hurrying through the open door, smiling, laughing, grateful for their rescue, for the warming sun. The cavalry came into view again, a portion of it swinging on westward, a smaller detail cutting away, slanting toward the stranded stagecoach and its passengers. A waxed-mustached major with a round, sunburned face came in ahead of his men, slowed, his eyes on the coach team.

"Corporal Hays!" he barked. "Catch up one of those stray mounts and hitch him into harness so these people can continue on their journey."

The officer moved in nearer to the house, halted. He saluted gravely and said: "Major Amos Allingham, at your service. We'll have you ready to move out in a few minutes. Pleased to see none of you has been seriously injured."

Allingham hesitated, looked over his shoulder to where three of his yellowlegs were getting the coach ready. A smile pulled at his lips. "Want to thank you for dispatching that young cowboy to us. We've been hunting those guerrillas for weeks. Got them all . . . every last one of them."

Mrs. Russell, once again a woman, began to weep softly and sought comfort in her daughter's arms.

Armstrong took a deep breath. "Was close," he said. "That young cowboy . . . did he get through all right? Without getting hurt, I mean."

The officer smiled again. "Well, from here to where we're bivouacked, it's around twenty miles. He rode the whole distance bareback and at a fast clip. He'll find standing most comfortable for a few days. Otherwise, he's fine. And by the way, Marshal," he added, swiveling his attention to Prince, "said he was your prisoner. Soon as he gave me the information I needed, he put himself in my custody. You'll find him waiting in my tent."

John Prince stared at the officer. Somewhere, deeply within his mind, a door opened, a wide door beyond which a pure white light shone brilliantly. He'd been wrong about Dave Kirby. There were others he'd been wrong about, too, most likely. And Kate — maybe he was wrong there. It was possible — no, probable. He could see that now. He'd been a fool, a great fool — and all that Mrs. Russell and Armstrong, the cattleman, had said he was.

He turned to them. There was a smile on his lips, the first they'd seen since he had boarded the stage.

"I'm glad Kirby got through. Took a lot of sand, and, when he goes before the judge in Rinconada, like for you to be there with us. Maybe if we all speak up, tell what he did, we can help things along for him a bit."

"Count on me," Armstrong said fervently.

Mrs. Russell bobbed her head. "I'll speak to my husband. Perhaps he can do something."

139

Prince swung back to Allingham. "Our thanks to you, too, Major, for getting here when you did."

"My job, sir," the officer said, and started to pull away.

"One more thing," John Prince called after him. "You have a telegraph wire connection at your camp?"

Allingham nodded. "Hooked in temporarily with the main line."

"Good. Like to send my wife a message, tell her I'll be home shortly."

Guns Along the Mimbros

Kinsey Ryan rode to the top of the ridge and halted, the buckskin fiddling impatiently as he pulled him in. Tugging at his wide-brimmed hat to cut down on the glare, he looked out over the vast Mimbros Valley country, a great, brown, and gray-green carpet unrelieved in its sun-seared texture except where Indian Creek laid a bright slash across its middle. Squarely in that center crouched the crumbling buildings of Strickland's Diamond S ranch, the faded giant of the past.

Turned restless by thoughts of failure in those times he had gone to reason with Jody Strickland, he rowled the buckskin into movement and started the slow descent of the cañon. This would be the last time he'd try to talk to her, Ryan told himself. If Jody felt as she did before, he'd drop it once and for all and forget about buying the Strickland place.

The going was hard and the gelding was showing lather long before he was near the bottom of the grade. It was due partly, he realized, to the sultriness. There was rain coming — something that would be most welcome to the country now lying parched and withered in the summer's driving heat.

141

Reaching level ground, he slowed to watch a flock of crows struggling across the sky, breaking the hush with their harsh cries, and then continued on until he was in the weedy yard fronting the ranch house. At once the door opened and Jody Strickland moved out into the open.

" 'Mornin'," he said, coming to a halt.

She stood quietly, a slender figure in faded denim and cotton shirt — and with an old carbine cradled in her arms. Sunlight glinted off the red-brown of her hair and her eyes were blue points of mistrust and suspicion. Ryan could count the times on one hand he'd see her in a dress. Tom Strickland, wanting a son and getting a daughter, had done his best to turn her into a boy, even to the point of naming her.

She nodded coolly. "What do you want?"

"Thought we might talk a mite," Ryan said. "Mind if I climb down?"

"Stay where you are," she said flatly.

Kinsey Ryan shrugged. A lanky, graying, old cowpuncher drifted up from the corner of the barn, took a position close by. A moment later he was joined by a second man, an aged Mexican. Ryan felt the sharp eyes of the pair fasten upon him. He had a moment then recalling the hours he'd spent with the two oldsters, listening to their tales of the early days. They'd been Tom Strickland's right and left arms — and once they'd been his idols, his friends. Now they were strangers.

Jody said: "If you've come again to make an offer, the answer's still the same. Diamond S is not for sale . . . not to you or anybody."

"All right, all right!" Ryan said in mild protest. "Thought maybe you'd been thinking it over. Need more grazing and a shorter way to get my herd to market. But if you won't sell, that settles it."

"Was settled a long time ago. Long as I've got Abner and Manuel, Diamond S will keep going."

Ryan stirred again. The buckskin stamped restlessly and the *caws* of more crows flying across the valley sounded faintly. The sweet smell of fresh hay was in the air and somewhere a dog was barking.

"No reason we can't be friends, Jody," Ryan said gently. "You ever need any help, call on me."

"You'll never see the day!" the girl snapped, a note of desperation in her voice. "I'll never let you or anybody else take my ranch away from me! Now . . . get out!"

An answer formed on Ryan's lips, but Abner Slocum's words, dry and firm, stopped it: "Move along, son. Move along now."

Ryan nodded curtly, swung about, and headed up the trail, slow anger burning within him. He'd known Jody since they were toddlers — and now he didn't know her at all. There simply was no understanding her. After the death of her father she seemed to think the whole world was out to skin her, take Diamond S from her . . . Well, he was through with it. If that was the way she wanted things, that's the way they would be.

He pulled up short, suddenly catching sight of two riders moving uptrail ahead of him and guessed immediately they had witnessed his conversation with the girl. When he reached the rim of the valley, they were waiting — Hugh Carson astride his showy, white gelding and Dan Pike on his gray.

Carson was a hard-driving sort of a man with but one ambition — to make his Seven X spread the largest in the territory. His land bordered Ryan's to the west, half encircling him, and twice Carson had made an offer to buy. Ryan knew, too, that Hugh had hopes of obtaining the Diamond S and realized what position this would put him in if it ever came to pass; he would be neatly pocketed in the merciless palm of Carson. But, remembering Jody's words of a few minutes past, he felt he need have no fear of that.

"You're a little off your range," Carson said as Ryan drew up.

Anger flooded through him at Hugh's unreasonable observation. He met the rancher's reserved glance, aware also of Pike's level stare. "Happens I go where I damn' well please."

"Sure . . . sure. Glad I run into you. Aimed to drop by your place."

"We've got nothing to talk about, Hugh."

"Figure we have. I'm offering to buy you out again. Needing more range . . . same as I need the Strickland place so's I can trim a week off trailing my herds to the railhead. Thought maybe you were ready to . . ."

"Wasn't ready the last time you brought it up. Don't figure I ever will be."

144

Dan Pike edged nearer. The gunman had an odd, flat way of looking at a man, and trouble lay across his features like a broad scar. "A long time," he murmured. "Take my advice, friend . . . sell out now."

Ryan raked Pike with a cold glance. "Take your advice and go to hell. I stay."

The faintest of smiles tugged at Carson's lips. "You'll move . . . one way or another," he said. "Might as well make it easy on yourself."

Anger again swept through Ryan. "That a threat?"

"Advice . . . like Pike said. Seven X is going to be the biggest ranch in the country. Bet on it."

"Not if you're counting on my land. You try anything with that girl and you'll have a fight on your hands."

"So I've got a fight on my hands," Carson said blandly. "You think I got big as I am without trouble?"

"Maybe," Dan Pike cut in, "we ought to open the ball right now. Where's your gun, friend?"

"Next time I'll be wearing it," Ryan said, and turned away, placing his back squarely to the two men. For the first few yards the hair on the back of his neck crawled, and then he shrugged off the tension. He had been caught defenseless; it was up to Pike and Carson either way you looked at it. They'd put a bullet in his back, or they wouldn't. It was that simple.

He gained the crest of the ridge up to which the trail led, dropped over the yonder side, breathed deeper. No bullets had come ripping into his body, tearing life from him.

But this is not the end of it, he thought, as he swung the buckskin toward his own range — *only the*

145

beginning. Hugh Carson had been building up to this day for a long time. A greedy man hungry for even more, he was making his first move and a dark and wild current had sprung to life in the Mimbros country. Peace was dead. From that moment on, violence would hang like a threatening shadow over the cañons and flats.

The next day, near the middle of the afternoon, he rode into his own yard and found Jody and the *vaquero*, Manuel, waiting. The Mexican slumped in his saddle, his dark, lined face betraying nothing, but the girl was tense. The old carbine, cocked and ready, was in her hands.

"I came after my stock," she greeted him flatly.

Ryan stared at her. "What stock?"

"Don't make out like you don't know!" she flared. "Been missing steers right along. Never thought it would be you."

Ryan was suddenly furious as understanding came to him. "You accusing me of rustling your cattle?"

"I am. Steers are over in your north quarter right now. Abner's with them. Were driven in last night, or maybe this morning."

Ryan's face was a mask of suppressed fury. "You think I had something to do with it?"

"Stock's on your range," Jody said. "And I think maybe you'd do anything to force me to sell . . ."

Ryan swore, dropped from his saddle, and stalked to the house. From the peg on the wall he took down his gun, strapped it on, taking a moment to check the

146

cylinder for loads. He was seething within and it showed in the hard glitter filling his eyes, in the quick, fluid action of his movements. How the cattle got onto his range he had no idea, but they'd be off damned quick.

"Let's go," he snapped, swinging back onto the buckskin.

They picked up Frank Sears, his foreman, halfway to the north line and Ryan put the question to him. Sears wagged his head.

"Didn't know they was on the place. Don't reckon Charlie Green seen them, either, 'cause he didn't say nothin' about 'em. Who found them?"

"The old one and me," Manuel said. "We follow the tracks when the sun comes this morning. The old one, he stay while I go for the *señorita*."

"Somebody drove 'em in late last night or early this mornin'," Sears said, shaking his head again. "Was over that way myself only yesterday."

An hour later they reached the arroyo where the cattle were pocketed — and nearby they found Abner Slocum. The old cowpuncher lay beside his horse, a bullet hole in his head. A cry wrenched from Jody Strickland's lips when she saw the crumpled shape, and then she lapsed into a stunned silence while Ryan and the others dismounted and examined Slocum.

"Dead a couple of hours," Frank Sears surmised. "Caught it straight on. Reckon he seen it comin'."

Grim, Kinsey Ryan drew himself upright, crossed to where the girl waited. He had no way of knowing who was behind the death of Abner or the clumsy attempt to make it appear he had been rustling Diamond S cattle, but he had a good idea. Regardless, the war had started.

"Jody," he said, halting beside the girl. "All hell's going to break loose around here now. Think it'd be a smart idea for you to move into town, put up at the hotel for a few days."

Her eyes flamed. "And just let you take over everything?"

"No . . . ," he said patiently, "I only mean . . ."

"I know what you mean!" she screamed. "You rustle my stock, bushwhack the kindest old man who ever lived . . . and now you want me to move off my place . . . leave it so's you . . ."

"You're loco!" Ryan exploded in a sudden burst of exasperation. "Wouldn't have that ranch of yours now as a gift! You're forgetting there're others who . . ."

"I'll go to town, all right!" Jody raged. "But for one thing . . . see the sheriff and have him arrest you for murder and rustling. You think you can get Diamond S away from me, think again!"

Abruptly she spurred away from Ryan, moved up to the old *vaquero.* "Manuel, put Abner across his saddle and take him home. I'll . . ."

"What's all that smoke?" Frank Sears broke in, pausing as he stepped up to help Manuel.

Ryan turned, looked toward the valley. A dark haze was billowing into the overcast sky, growing steadily and thickening with intensity. He flung a quick glance to Jody.

"Looks like your place!"

The girl paled under her tan. She stared at the ugly smudge for several minutes and then, wheeling about, raced off at a hard gallop. Instantly Ryan spun to his buckskin, vaulted to the saddle, and started in pursuit. Within a short distance he had caught up and together they sped across the rolling plains, but if Jody Strickland was aware of his presence, she gave no sign.

They reached the lip of the basin in which Diamond S lay, plunged recklessly down the grade. Ryan had hoped they would find nothing more serious than a grass fire, bad enough during the dry season, of course, but in this he was disappointed. The smoke, laced with tongues of flame, was coming from the Strickland quarters. He glanced at the heavy, dark clouds in the east. Rain was coming but it would not arrive soon enough to help.

Long before they reached the yard, they could see raw fire leaping from one of the barns. A half dozen men were running back and forth from the watering trough in futile efforts to check the blaze. Smoke rolled through the still air, and, when they finally reached the hard pack, the men had given up the attempt to kill the conflagration of the barn and were endeavoring to keep the flames from spreading farther.

Ryan sensed deep trouble when he slid from the buckskin. Of the men there, all but one were Seven X riders — counting Hugh Carson and Dan Pike. The motionless figure of another cowpuncher lay face down near the main house.

Jody halted before the singed, soot-streaked boy who did stable duty for her. "What happened?" she asked in a hopeless voice.

The boy rubbed at his face. "I see the smoke from the corral and I come quick. The barn was on fire. Mister Carson and his men were trying to put it out." He paused, pointed to the prone figure. "They tell me he start it."

"Who is he?" Jody said, frowning.

"I think," Hugh Carson drawled, moving up to her, "you'll find he works for Ryan."

Ryan came about slowly, seeing from the corner of his eye Dan Pike slide in next to Carson. He felt the sudden rise of tension and, ignoring Jody's stricken glance, walked stiffly to the dead man, turned him over. It was Charlie Green, one of his riders.

Hugh Carson's voice reached him. "We rode up just after he'd started the blaze. Made a run for his horse, but Pike cut him down before he reached it. Sorry we couldn't save the barn. One of your riders, ain't he, Ryan?"

Kinsey Ryan wheeled slowly, anger burning through him. He saw Dan Pike come alert and three of the other Seven X men close in quietly behind Carson. Within him a driving urge to draw his pistol, still Hugh Carson's lying, cunning tongue forever, surged upward. But he pressed it back. Against such odds he'd never get off a shot.

"He worked for me, but he never set that fire."

Dan Pike's cold voice was sharp. "You calling us liars, mister?"

150

"You're the best judge of that," Ryan said, ignoring caution, anger overriding reason.

Jody Strickland broke the breathless hush that followed. "Stop it . . . you hear? Stop it! I won't have any more killing . . ."

Hugh Carson bowed his head politely. "Of course. Now, Miss Strickland, if there's anything I can do . . . help . . ."

"Just go," Jody said wearily, and turned to Ryan: "You, too. Load up your man and get off my place. I . . . I'll let the sheriff handle this."

Ryan shrugged, moved quietly to where Charlie Green's horse stood. He led the animal to where the body of the young cowpuncher lay and with the aid of the stable boy hoisted it to the saddle, and then climbed aboard his buckskin. A low rumbling of thunder broke through the hot silence as he crossed the yard, and following it Hugh Carson's words to Jody came to him.

"Friends ain't always what they claim to be, but you can depend on me and Seven X, Miss Strickland. If it's help you're needing to rebuild that barn, just say the word and my boys'll be here. Or maybe you'd like to get out of the business. I'd be willing to pay . . ."

Ryan rode on. Hugh was having things all his way, and worst of all Jody seemed to be taken in by his smooth words. She should know better. While Hugh Carson was a comparative newcomer to the Mimbros country, just about everyone had him figured out.

He glanced to the darkening sky as thunder again rolled massively through the close heat. The storm was

151

much nearer now, a heavy thudding sounding quickly after each spurt of lightning. He glanced to the body of Charlie Green, draped across the saddle. Charlie had been a good man — certainly one who'd not have started a fire on Jody's property — or anyone else's, for that matter.

Nor had any of his hands slain old Abner Slocum or rustled any of Diamond S stock, but in the state of mind Jody was he could not make her see it. He could look to Hugh Carson for all of it — but proving it to Jody and others in the valley was something else. Hugh's word was equally good as his — perhaps better to those who benefited materially from Seven X patronage — but the truth was the truth and there should be a way of bringing it out. You'd think Jody could see Hugh was pursuing the old system of divide and conquer to obtain what he sought — both their ranches.

Frank Sears was waiting when he rode into the yard. Holding a lighted lantern above his head, he peered through the darkness. "Ain't that Charlie Green's horse?"

Ryan nodded. "Charlie's dead."

Sears noted the cowpuncher's body in that moment, stepped in close. He studied Green's face for a few moments, then: "Who done it?"

"Dan Pike . . . probably when Carson told him. Claimed they caught him setting fire to the Strickland place."

"Which'll be a god-damn' lie," Sears said quietly. He looked off toward the flats. "Reckon there ain't no stoppin' things now."

Placing the lantern on the ground, he stepped to Green's horse, began to untie the leather thongs that secured the body. When they were free, he lifted the cowpuncher, laid him gently to one side.

"Hold that lantern up!" Ryan said suddenly.

Sears threw him a puzzled look, picked up the light.

"Hold it close to the saddle skirt, there behind the cantle."

Frank Sears saw the dark stain, leaned closer, touched it with his fingers. "Blood. Charlie's, I reckon. Got him from behind . . ."

"That's it . . . they got him from behind but not while he was on the saddle," Ryan said in a quick way. "Hugh claims they shot him in Strickland's yard when he made a run for his horse!"

Sears scratched at his chin. "Don't hardly see . . ."

"Means they put a bullet in him somewhere out on the range, brought him in, and dumped him in Jody's yard. If it had been the way they said, there'd be no blood on the saddle."

The old foreman was nodding vigorously. "For a fact! Them murderin' skunks . . . probably done the same . . ."

"Take Charlie into town in the buckboard," Ryan cut in. "Then roust out the sheriff and bring him to Jody's. Meet you there."

"What're you figurin' to do?"

"Think maybe I can make Jody listen to me now. I aim to try, anyway. And I'm not trusting Hugh any where she's concerned, either. He'd as soon put a

153

bullet in her and blame it on me as he'd draw a breath. Got to see that she's safe."

Frank Sears bobbed his head. "All right, but don't you go takin' after that Seven X bunch alone. You wait for me and the sheriff."

"I'll wait," Ryan answered, and wheeled out of the yard.

The first spatter of rain lashed at him when he started down the long slope into the valley. Pausing, he untied his slicker, threw it over his shoulders, and moved on, going softly now that he was approaching the Diamond S. Carson, or some of his bunch, could still be around, and he was taking no chances. He must get to Jody, tell her the facts, and Hugh Carson equally unwilling to run any risks would do all in his power to keep him from doing so.

He came into the ranch house from its north side, halted in the shadows. The night was so dark he could distinguish little but there didn't appear to be any horses at the hitch rack or in the corral, although the fitful flashes of lightning afforded him little opportunity to be certain. After a time he drifted closer through the dripping blackness, pulled up again in a thicket of tamarisk near the kitchen door.

Dismounting, he started across the narrow space of open ground. Halfway a vivid flash of blue light flooded the land and he had a brief glimpse of the yard and nearby buildings. There was a horse or horses — he could not be sure which — near the bunkhouse. And he could not be certain if they belonged to Jody or Hugh Carson. It was too late to worry about it, anyway.

Drawing his pistol, he entered the house and, walking quietly, made his way through the hall to Jody's room.

He paused at the door, listened. There were no sounds coming from the yard and all was quiet within the house. Taking the knob in his hand, he twisted, flung the panel open, and stepped inside. Instantly he heard Jody gasp, saw her rise in alarm. He reached for her, clapped a hand over her mouth.

"Don't yell," he said in a husky whisper. "Not sure we're alone."

She nodded, and he released her. In the shadowy room he watched her pull away, turn to face him. Her voice was utterly cold. "What do you want?"

"Straighten this thing out," Ryan said, crossing to the window. Lightning flared, setting off the wet, glistening planes of his face, and the dripping of water from his hat and slicker was a muted pattering.

"No point in talking. The sheriff . . ."

"I've sent for him. Be here soon. Want you to listen while we're waiting. It's Hugh Carson that's behind everything that's happening around here. He wants your place, same as he wants mine, and he'll do anything to get them."

Jody shook her head. "You're not sure of that . . . you only think . . . or maybe you're just trying to clear yourself . . ."

"I've got proof that he lied about Charlie Green. He wasn't killed the way Hugh said. They shot him in the back somewhere, hauled him in, and dumped him in your yard. Then cooked up that yarn about the fire."

Jody was completely silent. The sky rumbled again, split with a jagged flash of light. He saw that she was looking directly — hopefully at him.

"Is . . . is that true, Kinsey? Can you prove . . . ?"

"I can prove it," Ryan said flatly. "Reason I sent for the sheriff. I figure when we come down on Hugh, shove that proof into his face he . . . or one of his bunch . . . will start talking, admit the other . . ."

Ryan's voice broke off. A noise, different from the shuddering of the storm against the house, had caught his attention. He motioned Jody back against the wall, moved away from the window.

"What is it?"

He shook his head, dissatisfied with what he knew, or what he did not know. But there had been something, and the little flags of warning within him were still waving. Cautiously he eased more to his left, getting away from Jody Strickland as far as possible, removing himself entirely from the scope of the windows.

The door kicked open suddenly. In the same fragment of time lightning shattered the darkness. Hugh Carson, wet clothing plastered to his thick body, eyes wild, legs spread, blocked the opening. A pistol was in each of his hands.

"Knew I was right!" he shrilled. "Told Pike you'd catch on . . . come here. Wouldn't listen. Something I never do . . . underestimate a man."

Ryan, moving constantly in order to offer no target in the darkness, struggled to make sense of Carson's words. Hugh seemed out of his mind, raving almost.

156

"Makes no difference, anyway," Carson went on. "Got you both now. In the same room. Be easy. Won't need Pike."

"Forget it, Hugh," Ryan said. "Drop your guns."

Carson fired at the sound of his voice but Ryan had already pulled aside. He triggered his own weapon, heard Carson gasp as the bullet smashed into him. Moving again, he waited, ready to fire a second shot. Lightning slashed through the curtain of blackness. Hugh Carson was buckling forward, arms hanging loosely at his sides. A small cry escaped Jody Strickland's lips from the far wall of the smoke-filled room, and then Dan Pike's voice, coming from the yard, reached Ryan.

"Hugh . . . you all right?"

Instantly Ryan wheeled. In a single stride he was through the doorway. A half dozen more carried him down the hallway to the kitchen door. Then, crouched low, he bolted into the open, plunged into the nearby tamarisk. Deep in the brush he waited for a flash of lightning that would point out the gunman's position. They would meet on equal terms now — and Jody was out of harm's way.

"Hugh . . . you hear me?"

"Hugh's dead," Ryan answered, lifting his voice above the wind and whipping rain. "Play it smart, Pike. Ride out and don't come back."

There was no reply. Ryan changed his position, edging closer to the lower end of the windbreak. The gunman was somewhere near the corral. He reached the edge of the brush, halted. Pike would be near, holding back, as was he, for the next break in the darkness.

Abruptly the yard was flooded with brilliant light. Ryan saw the half-bent shape of Dan Pike, fired even as the gunman triggered his weapon. Ryan spun half about, went to one knee as a bullet slammed into his shoulder. He righted himself, poised for another flash of lightning, pistol ready. Someone was yelling down near the bunkhouse and a lamp was showing against the window.

Again the night was split with a searing flash. Ryan's hand tightened about his weapon — and then eased off. Dan Pike lay sprawled face down in the mud, both arms out-flung. A long sigh slipped from Kinsey Ryan's lips as he pulled himself erect. Two or three men were hurrying up from the direction of the bunkhouse, all yelling questions. He scarcely heard them, conscious only of the tension draining from his body, the coolness of the rain pounding against his face.

"Kin?"

A slow smile cracked his mouth. Jody hadn't called him that for years. He turned, saw her standing on the narrow porch, a lamp in her hand.

"Are you all right?"

"I'm fine," he said, and moved toward her.

Reluctant Killer

On the crest of the last rise, Boyd Tripp drew rein and looked out over the vast spread of country unfurling below in an endless sea of tan and green. This was Idaho, lying peacefully in the broad shadows of the brooding Seven Devils Hills, this was the southern tip of Ten Mile Valley, sprawling warm and rich under a summer sun, and this was the end of a long trail — the homeland of Tom Nickerson, a man he'd traveled two thousand miles to kill. A river's bright slash traced across the valley's floor, meandering through thick willows, in and out among the trees, and Boyd Tripp's mind went back to his boyhood, to the words of an old spiritual he had heard his ma sing countless times — "One more river, one more river to cross . . . ," it went. Funny thing, he thought, that he should remember that old song just then. But it certainly was appropriate. Tom Nickerson lived somewhere across that small stream.

Boyd swung stiffly down from the saddle. He was weary and his muscles and joints ached from the endless hours on the trail. Cheyenne had been a long ride and the gauntness lying upon his lean young face

159

was like a stiff mask, giving him the appearance of being much older than his nineteen years.

After tying the bay horse to a clump of brush, he stretched, squared his wide shoulders, and sauntered to the slanted side of a low butte. He leaned back against its cool surface. A sigh came from him as a vagrant breeze, drifting down from the knobs and high cañons, riffled over him, touching him and turning him languorous and at ease. And for a time he was a young boy again and not a man bent to grim purpose.

His ma's song rocked gently through his mind again and he shrugged impatiently, wanting to cast it off. He needed no reminder of what lay ahead. Jack's pistol, holstered on his hip and thronged snugly to his leg, never allowed him to forget it. Its weight was a sullen, intangible force that had pushed and prodded him relentlessly along the desolate, dusty byroads of the territories for nearly two years now, never letting him rest, binding him to a search that had led from town to town, from ranch to ranch.

His sole purpose during those two years — to kill Tom Nickerson. Thinking about it, he shuddered involuntarily. To kill anything, much less another human being, was against his nature. He liked to see things grow, to put seed in the moist earth and watch a young plant spring forth to face the sun. It pleasured him to coax a spindle-legged calf into a husky, shaggy-coated steer, and he wished mightily that he was back on their little ranch in New Mexico right at this moment — his ranch now — tending the garden, and looking after the few head of cattle they had acquired.

He reckoned now he wouldn't even mind the chore of hauling water for the trees he'd planted.

But a man had obligations; Jack had drilled that into him. You looked after your own kith and kin, and you righted any wrongs done them without crying to somebody else. That's the way Jack said a man lived, and Jack knew. He was a wise one, that Jack — a man among men. Thus, when a bullet from the gun of some cowboy named Tom Nickerson had felled him, Boyd Tripp recognized his duty and saw clearly what had to be done. He had to find Nickerson and kill him.

He stirred, turned restless by the thought of what was ahead. At that moment he saw movement far below, near the water. A girl emerged from the thicket and plunged into the river. She began to frolic and swim. Caught up between curiosity and a vague feeling of embarrassment, he watched.

It was too great a distance to tell much about her, other than the fact that she was young and well-finished, and, when she had completed her swim and ducked back into the willows, he mounted the bay and drifted down the long slope to her. She had finished dressing and was winding the glinting damp folds of her hair into a bun when he pulled up.

Touching the brim of his cow-country hat, he said: "Afternoon, ma'am. Name's Boyd Tripp. You from around here?"

She regarded him thoughtfully for a moment, having her wonderment at his sudden appearance. He met her gaze, his eyes telling her nothing of the things he knew she would like to know. But, then, he had never paid

161

much attention to girls. The ones he had known back home, the Dollarhide twins who were neighbors ten miles to the south, were both spindly, knobby little creatures who always reminded him of freshly foaled colts, and he hadn't troubled to look at them twice. And during the past two years, on the trail, he was too busy with his quest.

But this girl moved him strangely. She had the deepest blue eyes he had ever seen, almost black. She was slim but well-curved, and her skin was the color of rich cream. She had a wide, full mouth and her dark hair glistened in the sunlight like the bangles cut from tin cans and hung on a Christmas tree.

He heard her say in answer to his question: "Yes, up the valley a way."

He pulled his gaze aside, shifting to the distance beyond the river. Almost reluctantly he asked: "Know a man named Tom Nickerson?"

She nodded at once. "Are you a friend of his?" she wanted to know.

"Not exactly," he finally said. "I've never met the man myself."

The girl was surveying him with frank interest. "You'll like Tom," she told him, ". . . and his wife, Nan. They have a little daughter."

Boyd Tripp staggered, the gesture an unconscious answer to his own thoughts rather than to her words. He had not known that Tom Nickerson was a family man. That was too bad. But it did not alter the fact that Jack was dead.

She asked: "You from cattle country?"

He nodded. "Down New Mexico way. Have my own spread. Haven't seen much of it lately, though. Been on the move a couple of years."

She studied him closely. "Drifter," she murmured finally, expressing in that one word a vast amount of womanly scorn for imperfection.

Boyd Tripp smiled grimly. "Maybe not after today," he said.

In the silence that followed, she swung onto her pony and began smoothing first the wrinkles from her corduroy skirt, and then straightening the cuffs of her white shirt-waist.

"There a town some'eres?"

She nodded. "Muleshoe's down the road a piece. I'm riding that way if you'd care to come along."

He wheeled the bay in beside her and they rode in quiet across the narrow bridge and along the willows until at least they broke into the open and a scatter of sun-grayed buildings lay before them. A few stores, a saloon or two, a livery barn and blacksmith shop, and a two-storied hotel bearing the faded sign **THE NORTHWEST** comprised Muleshoe.

They came to a halt and she asked: "Are you staying here?"

Boyd said: "I'll put up at the hotel." He paused, eyeing her with a half smile. "I don't recollect you telling me your name."

"It's Margaret . . . Margaret Grant. We'll meet again if you plan to see the Nickersons. I go there often. Good bye."

He touched the brim of his hat and watched her ride off. Sober, bitter thoughts suddenly moved in to crowd out the lightheartedness he had felt while they were together. What would she think of him if she knew his business with her friend Tom Nickerson?

When Margaret Grant had turned the corner from sight, Boyd Tripp rode to the hotel, dismounted, and tied the bay. Crossing the pine-floored porch where half a dozen old men sat in tipped-back chairs, enjoying their tobacco and memories, he entered the dusty lobby of The Northwest. A bald-headed clerk watched him approach the desk with round, expressionless eyes. Without speaking, the clerk pushed forward a pencil and dog-eared register.

Tripp wrote — **Boyd Tripp, Quemado, New Mexico** — in a hard, slanting hand, and asked: "How do I get to the Nickerson place?"

The clerk, glancing first at the book, gave him directions, and then slid a key across the counter.

Tripp murmured — "Later." — and re-crossed the lobby to the street. Stepping to the saddle of the bay, he rode in an easterly direction, filled suddenly with a pressing urgency to get the chore over with. He wanted to be done with it, to fulfill his obligation to Jack, and then perhaps he could think of other things — such as Margaret Grant, and picking up the loose threads of his own life.

After he had left the town, he drew his pistol, checked its cylinder for loads, and tested its action. Satisfied, he returned the gun to its holster and rode on. A short time later he came into the Nickersons' yard and drew rein before a low, rambling structure of hewn logs. Keeping a tight grip on his nerves, stifling the sickness he felt for what he had to do, he dismounted, walked quickly to the door, and knocked.

The door was opened by a woman of perhaps thirty. Blonde hair spilled down about the cameo-clean features of her face, and her eyes were soft and dark. Ann Nickerson had been a beauty once, but the hardships of frontier life were having their way, were leaving their definite mark.

A tot of a girl tugged her calico skirt, looking up at Boyd Tripp with mild interest.

The woman smiled at Tripp. "Yes?"

"Looking for Tom Nickerson," Tripp stated bluntly. "Does he live here?"

Something very like fear erased the smile from the woman's face. A ragged sort of anxiety appeared as if she might be recognizing danger in the presence of the tall, young stranger. For a long moment she hesitated.

"He lives here," she said finally. "But he's not home today. He's away."

"Will he be back today?"

"I . . . I don't know. I'm not sure."

He felt the steady pressure of her gaze, searching, probing, seeking an answer to some question she alone knew. A slight break in her voice betrayed her feelings.

"Who shall I say wanted to see him?"

Boyd Tripp shook his head. "Never mind. I'll come back another time."

He saw then that she was really afraid. She was guessing his purpose and he felt sorry for her. A

165

woman's intuition was a wondrous thing, and it would be sad for her and the child. But it had to be done. A life for a life, that's what Jack had drilled into him, and that was the way it would be — Tom Nickerson's life in payment for that of Jack. But it was too bad the woman and little girl would have to suffer.

Abruptly he swung about, mounted the bay, and rode back to Muleshoe.

Stabling his horse and leaving instructions for his care, Tripp went to his room in The Northwest. It was little different from hundreds of others he had paused in briefly during his wanderings — dirty, ill-furnished, ill-kept, and depressing. He sank down on the protesting iron bedstead, stretching out full length and giving way at last to weariness.

He lay motionless, not fully asleep or awake, but drifting in that in-between void where background and demands were old and familiar, but where Margaret Grant was a new figure. She watched him with sad, troubled eyes that held no understanding for him as he walked the dusty street of Muleshoe, gun in hand, to kill Tom Nickerson. But she must understand!

That conclusion brought him bolt upright, and fully awake. He must make her see what he had to do, that it was his duty and he could not shirk it. Surely she could see his side of it!

He would make her see, he thought. He rose at once, stripped off, and scrubbed down from the china bowl and pitcher. After shaving, he donned clean clothes and went downstairs to the dining room where he was a lone customer. He ate slowly, enjoying his food, and, when he had finished, he got up, passed through the lobby under the curious eyes of the clerk, and headed for the stable.

Picking up the bay and getting directions from the hostler, he rode off through the cool twilight toward the Grant homestead. A breeze had sprung up from the nearby hills and already the stars were beginning to show, faint sparks of light in the darkening sky, but soon to be definite and exceptionally low-hanging.

The Grant place, he found, lay east of the settlement in a slashed-out clearing. The buildings were all bright and sharp in a new coat of white paint, outlined distinctly against the crowding circle of green growth beyond them. He paused at the gate in the rail fence, having a lonely man's appreciation for the scene. The fields were lush and soft; sweet freshness hung in the air like a heady perfume. Somewhere a man pounded on an anvil and overhead a straggle of noisy crows were etched in blackness against the clouds, bound for their roost for the night.

A door slammed and Margaret Grant came out on the full-length porch that spanned the building. She stood watching him. He rode down the lane and halted, awaiting her invitation.

"Hello," she said. "Won't you get down?"

He hesitated a moment, studying her smile, looking at the way the cotton dress molded her figure, and the way the last spray of sunlight glanced from her hair and put a sparkle in it. He nodded and dismounted, tethering the bay at the rail.

"Find the Nickerson place?"

"Yes," replied Tripp. "But he wasn't at home."

He moved up to stand before her, a tall, lean young man with wide shoulders. Removing his hat, he said: "Will you talk a spell with me?"

"Of course," she replied at once. "Let's sit on the edge of the porch."

When they were comfortable, sitting side-by-side, Boyd Tripp, ever direct and to the point, said: "Figured I'd better be telling you why I'm here. Like as not you won't be caring to see me again after you know."

"Oh?" she said, looking sideways at him.

He waited a long, dragging moment, then turned to face her. "I'm going to kill Tom Nickerson."

He heard the sharp intake of her breath, saw her eyes widen in shocked surprise. He waited out her breathless pause, wondering what her next words would be, if there would be any words at all.

In a shaken, outraged voice, she asked: "Why . . . why do you want to do that?"

Tripp's answer was flat, toneless. "He killed my brother Jack. Shot him down. I've been two years tracking him and now I've caught up with him."

She still sat beside him, looking straight ahead. But he felt her draw away from him.

"It's hard to believe," she said in a low voice. "I don't see how Tom Nickerson could ever hurt anybody. And you . . . you don't seem like a killer."

"A man doesn't always have a choice. Sometimes he has to do what he hates."

She faced him. "I don't understand that! If you don't want to do it . . . why are you?"

168

"Jack was all of the family I had left," he replied, remembering. "After the folks were killed by Indians, we were left to run the ranch together. He was ten years older than me but we got along fine. It was a good life. Hard, but good. Maybe Jack didn't like to work the place too much, but that was all right with me. When he would all of a sudden get restless and ride off, I knew he'd be back. He always returned, always bringing me something I'd wanted and having a new story to tell about his trip. Jack was a good man and nobody ever said he wasn't. Everybody liked him. Women, too, I reckon, because he was big and tall and always dressed fine. And he rode a coal-black horse with a silver-trimmed saddle. Then one day he left and didn't come back. Instead, a marshal from the next town brought me his horse and gun. Told me a man named Tom Nickerson had killed my brother. I raised what money I could and started looking for this Nickerson. I've found him."

Tripp paused, and after what seemed a long time Margaret Grant said wearily: "And to right one wrong, you are going to commit another terrible wrong."

"I have to," Tripp said doggedly. "He killed Jack. Now he will have to face up to me."

She got slowly to her feet. He followed suit and stood with his hat in his hand. "I was hoping you could understand what I've got to do," he said.

She shook her head. "Never! Never could I understand it. You idolized your brother, I can see that. But I can't see why you must become a killer for him."

"Tom Nickerson has to pay for what he did."

She whirled to him. "Why must he? Why must you take vengeance into your own hands?"

He shrugged, suddenly helpless before her question. "Because that's the way it is," he answered lamely. "A man has to look after his own people."

She stared at him, angry tears brightening her eyes. Some inward struggle was tearing at her, striving to make itself heard, but the words would not come to her lips. She uttered — "Oh!" — and, turning about, hurried across the gallery into the house.

Silently Boyd Tripp moved to the bay. He swung up, and rode from the yard. He did not feel like sleep and an hour or so later he drew up on the southern rim of Ten Mile Valley, near the point where he had halted earlier in the day.

Indecision was pressing him cruelly and the first doubt as to the right and wrong of things was gnawing at his mind, placed there by Margaret Grant. But that was only a woman's way of thinking, he assured himself. A man would think as Jack did — and demand the penalty from Nickerson that he was demanding.

Looking out over the vast bowl that was Ten Mile Valley, he watched the yellow squares of light wink out, one by one, as the minutes passed and it grew later. Most men took for granted the fine things of life they possessed such as those homes, small and large, scattered out beneath the star-broken sky. Only a few realized what it was like to sit alone on a hilltop and gaze out across an endless prairie, watching the friendly lights go out in another man's castle.

170

How many knew what it was like to live on the outer fringe, never fully beyond yet never actually within a world of people and activities and commonplace happenings? Only a few knew the summer-baked stuffiness of a cheap hotel room, or had lain awake listening to a bitter wind shouldering its unfriendliness against a ramshackle building in the dead of bleak winter. Many men, possessing the good and full things of life, lived and died without ever becoming aware of that void in which others existed.

Boyd Tripp knew. From the day Jack was killed there had been nothing else. It had been as if he were born anew to forsake the things he loved and become a lonely, wandering shadow, troubled and weary in a friendless universe.

It was close to midnight when he returned to the hotel and entered the lobby. The clerk, observing his arrival, glanced up.

" 'Evenin', Mister Tripp," he said in a carrying tone.

At once a tall, gray man rose from a chair in the lobby and crossed to meet Boyd.

"I'm Tom Nickerson," he said. "I understand you've been looking for me."

Tripp became a rigid figure. His jaw hardened into a sharp angle and light spilling from the overhead lamp struck against his cheek bones, mirroring off the tight skin. He stared at the man who had murdered his brother — the man he had hunted so long.

Nickerson surprised him. He was no cold-faced gunman, no dangerous-looking killer. From all

171

indications, he was just another man, ordinary, average, with an air of friendliness about him.

Doubt again assailed Tripp's mind, and he remembered how violently opposed Margaret Grant had been to this. He wondered: Could he be wrong in demanding this man's life in payment for his brother's? Could he be wrong and could Margaret Grant be right?

Into his mind's eye appeared a vision of Jack as he had last seen him — handsome Jack Tripp, sitting proud and straight in that devil-may-care way of his on the black stallion, with the sun shining on the silver mountings of his saddle. Indecision faded from Boyd's mind before that cherished memory.

"I've been looking for you," he stated harshly. "And you know why."

Nickerson did not flinch. "I suppose. Any use telling my side of the story?"

"None whatever," Tripp snapped. "You killed my brother. I'm here to square that or get killed trying."

Nearly complete silence lay across the hotel's lobby, the only sound being the clerk's strained, raspy breathing.

"You armed?"

Nickerson shook his head. "Don't wear one nowadays."

"Then put one on. We'll settle this in the morning."

The tall man nodded and Tripp swung by him, closing him out. He heard the wind go out of Nickerson in a long, despairing sigh and passed on up the stairway to his room. He entered, locked the door, and remained standing near it, momentarily held by his own reaction.

Often he had considered this very moment, wondering how he would feel when the time came to kill Tom Nickerson. He was not nervous and there was no fear raking through him, and for that he was thankful. He knew that he was better than average with a gun, for Jack had taught him the tricks of a quick, sure draw. Nickerson was undoubtedly good, but Boyd did not think the man would be better. No, it was not that he questioned his ability to stand against Tom Nickerson, nor was there any doubt he would emerge from the affair alive. It was simply the problem of whether he was right or wrong, a matter he had never considered until Margaret Grant placed it in his head. Until then, he had known he was right. Now he was unsure.

Moving away from the door, he sat down on the edge of the bed, all at once very tired. He lay back, not bothering to remove his clothing, while he struggled to clear his mind of all the conflicting thoughts.

A knocking brought him up, and he was amazed to see sunlight streaming through the window. His first guess was that Tom Nickerson stood outside, that he had perhaps brought the law with him to halt the gun play. But he dismissed that thought at once. Nickerson was not the sort of man who would run for help.

Boyd got to his feet, drew his gun, and turned the key in the lock.

It was Margaret Grant who entered. Her eyes ran over his tense figure, grasping the coiled readiness of his tall body, and recognizing the dark threat. Closing the door, she placed her shoulders against it, her face going tired and hopeless.

"This is the way it will always be," she said in a dead voice. "Always facing the door with a gun in your hand . . . always wondering who will come through it."

Tripp holstered his pistol.

"No," he said. "I didn't expect you. I did him. There'll be no others after Tom Nickerson."

"You think it will end there?" she cried. "You believe you can take a man's life and just forget it . . . that others will forget, too?"

"There won't be any others," he repeated doggedly. "This is between Nickerson and me. When it's done with and settled, it's ended."

She was a small, definite shape standing against the door. Her eyes were bright with worry and her voice carried a strong urgency. "It will never end, Boyd! Can't you see? You kill Tom and somebody else will come looking to kill you . . . somebody with revenge in his heart, or just some man wanting to build his reputation. It never stops!"

His shoulders slumped a little, but he said: "No, it won't be that way."

"It's not in you to kill," she hurried on, pressing the point. "Why must you turn yourself into a killer just because of some foolish sense of duty to your brother?"

Tripp stared at her. "There's nothing foolish about it. It's something I have to do. There's no way out for me."

174

"There is a way out," she said. "Just don't go out in that street and meet Tom Nickerson. He will be glad if you don't . . . and so will many others, including me." She hesitated, then added: "It . . . it means everything to me, Boyd. Just . . . just as you do. Tell me you will give it up."

He could only marvel at all the wondrous promise of her thus revealed. But the image of Jack Tripp stood beyond her, and he knew there could be no compromise.

"I'm sorry, Margaret," he said in an empty voice, dead hollow with regret.

A small cry of despair escaped her lips, but he dropped his head and did not look up. He heard the slight, feminine rustle of her as she turned and opened the door. He heard her whisper — "Good bye." — with utter finality, in a voice as faint as willow dust, and then she was gone. Gone forever, he knew.

Muleshoe lay hushed and tense under the slowly climbing sun. Boyd guessed, at once, that Nickerson had already put in an appearance, that he was somewhere close by. Checking his gun, he stepped off the hotel porch and started for the stable at the far end of the street. Somewhere in between he would find Nickerson.

He moved at a slow, deliberate pace. Sweat began to build up under his hatband, gathering on his forehead, but he did not scrub it away. Jack had once told him, in such a situation, to let nothing distract him. "Keep your mind on your business," Jack had warned. Only vaguely

175

did Boyd hear the muted, suppressed sounds that hung in the throttled air — the ragged sobbing of a child somewhere, the stamp of a restless horse, the far-distant barking of a dog.

But even as he paced slowly up the street, he could not keep Margaret Grant from his thoughts. Her words kept stabbing at him, jarring, setting up their questions and their doubts. How could he be wrong? A man had a right to settle such things in the way all other men considered right. Jack had always said a man did such things as a matter of honor, of principle. Then how could he be wrong?

A thought came to him suddenly. Perhaps he should have let Nickerson talk last night in the hotel lobby. Maybe he ought to hear his side of the story. Margaret might even feel differently about it if all of the facts were known. He halted. There was still time for it. He would tell Nickerson to go ahead and . . .

Tom Nickerson came out of the stable and advanced to meet him. The man's hands were lifted well away from his body and he came to a stop some fifteen yards from Boyd. His face was frozen, a long, melancholy mask of gray, and his eyes, squinted against the sun, were steady and direct.

"I'm ready," he said through the leaden hush.

Tripp watched him closely, alert for any tricks. Tom Nickerson was good, no doubt about that. He would have to be to shoot down Jack. Jack was one of the best.

"You had in mind doing some talking last night," he began.

176

A shrill cry at the edge of the street sliced through his words. Nan Nickerson broke suddenly from a doorway and came running to her husband.

"Tom! I won't let him do it!" She was near screaming. "I won't let him kill you!"

Nickerson took her gently by the shoulders and tried to put her aside. She broke free and started running toward Boyd Tripp, her blonde hair disarranged and streaming down her back. Halfway, she stumbled and fell. She struggled up and came on.

"You're wrong . . . you're wrong about Jack!" she cried. "You didn't know him at all! He was bad and cruel!"

Tripp stiffened as the words beat against him. He had a fleeting vision of his brother astride the great black stallion, riding off like a shining knight in one of the story books at home. And then, unaccountably, the picture began to blur, to tarnish and fade.

"He promised to marry me, but he went off and left me," Nan Nickerson sobbed, crying out her secret for all to hear. "He never came back. He didn't even send word, or write. Tom married me to give my baby a name and give us a home. Do you hear, Boyd Tripp? Your brother was bad! When he did return, he wouldn't leave me alone. He tried to make me run off with him and leave my husband and baby . . . but I wouldn't go. Then, when he still wouldn't leave me alone, Tom killed him."

Boyd Tripp watched the woman sink exhaustedly into the street's dust. He looked at her for a moment and in that moment something deep inside him,

177

something cold and brutal, died. And a vision, long-cherished, was shattered in his mind's eye like a pebble breaking the surface of a pool of calm water.

He turned away. A tremendous load had lifted from his shoulders. He was a free man once again, and to the free belongs the future. He scanned the street, searching for Margaret Grant. And he saw her, waiting on the porch of the hotel.

A Place for Danny Thorpe

He came from the blue-shadowed mountain and deep-valleyed country of New Mexico, from the long, glittering flats of Arizona, from Texas, from Kansas — from everywhere almost and had yet to find his place in the scheme of things. In San Francisco he thought the search had ended, but again failure in the shape of Nate Tobin — Nugget Nate Tobin, the gambling king — had overtaken him. Now he was on the run, fearing for his life.

In the black shadows of Montgomery Street, he flattened himself against the clammy wall of a building and peered into the misty darkness. Newton and Stanger, two of Tobin's plug-uglies, were out there somewhere, silent, vengeful shadows still dogging his steps, still thirsting for his blood. Scarcely breathing, he waited, listened. Off in the direction of the Bay a ship hooted, a lost, lonely sound in the fogbound night.

In the beginning Danny Thorpe had dreamed of being a rancher. Since he was Texas born and raised, it was a natural desire but in that broad land of tall and powerful men it soon became apparent to him that he was a misfit, a boyman no one ever took seriously. Eventually it set him to drifting and he moved from one

179

territory and state to another, astray in a heedless world where his diminutive stature was continually a handicap that denied him the opportunities for which he so eagerly hungered.

Finally San Francisco, where he had heard jockeys were in demand and there was good money to be made at the racetracks . . . It had started well. He had a way with horses that brought out the best in them. In a few weeks he was recognized as one of the peers — and then Nate Tobin had stepped in. He ordered Danny to lose a certain race, voiced dire threats if he did not. Danny played it straight and his mount won easily. Tobin dropped a small fortune and quickly sent Pete Newton and Bill Stranger, two of his prize killers, to make an example of the little man who dared defy him. Danny Thorpe fled, aware of his great danger, aware, too, of another failure. He was . . .

"Got to be right along here somewheres."

Stanger's voice cut through the muffled night. Danny drew closer to the wall, his nerves taut, heart racing. They were moving in and there was nothing he could do but wait — and hope. He had no weapon of any kind with which to defend himself, not even a pocket knife. The pistol he had once owned had been sold long ago when cash ran low.

"Ain't so sure." Newton's reply was couched in doubt. "Could've turned the other way. Sure ain't seeing no signs of him."

"He's here," Stanger said stubbornly. "Just stand quiet for a spell and listen."

Guarding his breath, Danny rode out the dragging moments. The ship in the harbor hooted again and somewhere a horse trotted over cobblestone pavement, the hoof beats faint and hollow-sounding. Saliva gathered in his mouth and he swallowed hard. Despite the coolness of the night, sweat lay thickly on his brow and he fought the urge to wipe it off.

A wave of frustration and anger surged through him. Why did such things always have to happen to him? Why could he never find a decent job, live an ordinary life as did other men? Why did something always happen to upset things just as he was getting set? He was finished in San Francisco, and in horse-racing, thanks to Nate Tobin, whose tentacles reached far to touch and encircle the sport. He would have to move on, look for a different way to live. But what — and where?

He groaned silently at the prospect; he had tried about everything. There was little, if anything left. And then, suddenly, he recalled a newspaper advertisement he had read. At the time he had thought little of it; now he brought it back to mind:

WANTED

Young, skinny, wiry fellows. Not over 28. Must be expert riders willing to risk death daily. Orphans preferred. Wages $25 per week. Apply Central Overland Express.

181

The Pony Express! It had begun operation just that spring, carrying mail between Sacramento and St. Joseph, Missouri. Maybe he could get on with them. His spirits lifted as this ray of hope broke through his despair. There was a company office in San Francisco, but that, of course, was out; he could not risk being spotted by Tobin's thugs. The division point was Sacramento, he had heard. He could go there, apply for a job. Sacramento was a good ninety miles away, but there were always freight wagons on the road, and, if a man worked it right, he could always hitch a ride.

He could do all that, he thought grimly, if he could stay alive — could give Stanger and Newton the slip. Desperately he began to search his mind for an idea, for some means of escape. There must be a way — there had to be.

"I'm telling you, he ain't here." Newton's words came unexpectedly from the darkness a dozen paces to his right. "He headed the other way. I'm betting on it."

"You're betting on it," Stanger said mockingly. "Man needs a reason to bet . . ."

"Heard a noise over there a bit ago. Could've been him."

"Could've been you dreaming."

"Naw. Reckon I know what I heard."

A small tremor raced up Danny Thorpe's spine as an idea lodged in his mind. Pete Newton thought he had detected a sound down the street in the opposite direction; perhaps, if he made it definite, proved him right . . . Danny reached for his hat, moving his arm carefully to avoid the rustle of cloth. He took the small-brimmed headpiece in his hand, raised it high, and sent it sailing off into the night. It struck against some obstacle, set up a soft disturbance.

"There!" Newton said instantly. "You hear that?"

"I did," Stanger admitted grudgingly. "Come on. Let's have a look."

Danny listened to the soft scraping of the men's boots as they turned, walked toward the source of the sound. Waiting no longer, he wheeled, and, resisting the urge to run, he moved carefully and quietly to the far corner of the block. Once there, he gave in to the need to hurry. With luck he would find a freighter rolling north before he reached the edge of town.

Four weeks later, astride a horse lent him by bitter-tongued old Pat McCoskey, Express line superintendent at Sacramento, he was on the way to Smith's Crossing, in mid-Nevada. In his pocket was his assignment to the post which would be his home station; behind him lay seventeen days of intensive training in the art of being a Pony Express rider. And further in the past were Nate Tobin and all the other symbols of failure that had haunted him. That was all over now for at last he had found himself, his place. It remained only for him to prove his abilities to McCoskey and the job was his permanent property.

It had not been easy to endure the lash of the superintendent's haranguing, but he had stayed with it, stubbornly refusing to lose heart. After taking the oath required of all riders — not to swear or drink liquor while on duty, always to conduct himself as a

183

gentleman, and never abuse the horseflesh — he gave himself over to McCoskey, who hammered relentlessly at him day and night.

"Bend your knees, god dammit!" the old man shouted at him time after time when he was having difficulty dismounting from a running horse. "You'll be breaking your legs first out, iffen you don't!"

And Danny Thorpe had learned, just as he had become proficient in handling the *mochila*, an ingenious leather blanket designed to fit over the saddle and upon which four mail pouches had been stitched. It was loaded at each end of the run, was then passed from rider to rider, the trick being to make the exchange without loss of time.

"Nine days from here to Saint Joe!" McCoskey had told him. "That's what we're shooting for. We're doing it in ten now . . . and that's less than half what it takes a letter to come by boat or stagecoach. But we want it done in nine . . . and we sure as hell can do it if you blasted saddle-warmers'll work at it!"

"Be doing my best," Danny had replied, continually awed by McCoskey's enthusiasm and utter devotion to the cause. "I'll try . . ."

"Best ain't always good enough. Got to do better. And time's not the only thing important, either. That mail's got to get through . . . come perdition, it's got to get through! You understand that? No matter what . . . you get your *mochila* to the next station so's the link rider can keep it moving. We don't take no excuses . . . none."

"Yes, sir. All I'm asking is a little luck . . ."

184

"Luck!" McCoskey exploded. "Man makes his own luck, and don't you forget it! You just mind what I've been telling you and you won't need to depend on something like luck."

And thus it had gone until McCoskey, finally satisfied although frank in declaring himself unconvinced, sent him on his way. Now, with a warm, late fall sun caressing his shoulder, he gained the last rise and looked down on what he hoped would be his new home, Smith's Crossing.

In appearance it left much to be desired. It was no more than a thin scatter of gray, sun- and wind-scoured buildings and pole corrals, completely devoid of vegetation except for a lone tree that stood in solitary dejection in front of the largest structure.

The past was far behind Danny Thorpe when he pulled to a halt at the hitch rack in front of the mud-chinked, log-cabin office of the Pony Express and dismounted. He paused for a time, studying the sign above the doorway, a serious-faced miniature of a man dressed in black cord pants, knee-high boots, fringed buckskin coat, and rumpled porkpie hat. Heavier woolen clothing, suggested by Pat McCoskey, was rolled inside the poncho and behind the cantle of his saddle.

Hitching at the holstered gun — also borrowed from the line's superintendent — slung at his hip, he crossed to the doorway and entered. Again he halted, allowed his eyes to adjust to the abrupt change of light. It was a huge room, he saw, with little furniture that was covered with a thin veneer of yellow dust. Someone was rattling dishes in a room that turned off the primary area and the good, inviting odor of coffee hung in the still, warm air like tantalizing perfume.

"Reckon you're Thorpe, the new rider," a voice said from the left.

Danny wheeled, confronted a squat, dark man with close-set eyes and a friendly grin. "That's me," he said, and produced the letter McCoskey had given him. "You'd be Wylie Courtright, the station agent."

Courtright nodded. He opened the letter, glanced at it, thrust it into his pocket. "Had word from Mac that you'd be here today. Good thing. You'll have to make the run in the morning."

"Suits me," Danny said, glancing involuntarily toward the kitchen.

"Expect you're a mite hungry," the agent said, missing nothing. "Sit yourself down and I'll see what I can rustle up. Then we'll talk."

Danny settled himself at a table near a window. From there he could see the corral in which a dozen or so horses stood, hipshot in the pleasant sunlight. All were rough, hard-planed little animals that looked as though they could withstand any amount of punishment heaped upon them. Farther on was the blacksmith shop. The double doors were open and red coals glowed in the forge like evil eyes. Presently the smithy began to work his anvil, the ringing of his hammer clean and clear in the long-reaching quiet.

Courtright reappeared bringing a sandwich of bread and cold beef, cups, and a small granite pot of coffee. "Ought to hold you till supper," he said, and sat down

186

opposite. "How's things in Sacramento? Old Mac still pawing the earth like always?"

Danny grinned between bites. "He's sure one for the book, all right."

"Don't think he'd be satisfied even with that feller on the winged horse," the agent said, wagging his head. "But he's got the right idea. Training he gives you boys is what's making this mail line work."

"Thought I was a pretty fair hand with a horse until I came up against him," Danny said. "What's my other home station and how far is it?"

"Red Valley . . . and it's about a hundred and seventy miles off. You got eleven relay stations in between."

"A hundred and seventy miles," Danny murmured. "Quite a piece."

"For a fact. Most home stations are about a hundred, more or less. This stretch's the longest on the line. That's why we have trouble keeping a man on it. But it ain't too bad. Mostly flat country and easy going."

"Any Indian trouble?"

"Not lately. Country's too dang' god-forsaken even for them, I expect. Personally I don't blame a man for quitting it."

"I'll stick," Danny said, "if I make the grade."

Courtright was silent for a moment. Then: "Don't think you'll have any trouble doing that. Just keep remembering that mail's got to come through on time . . . but mostly it's got to come through. I reckon Mac told you all that."

"He sure did . . . plenty loud and often."

"That's sort of extra special now. You're going to be carrying some mighty important mail in your *mochila* on your return trip."

Danny frowned, poured himself a second cup of coffee. "Important?"

"Yeah, the election returns. People'll be real anxious to know who won . . . Lincoln or that feller Douglas."

Danny had forgotten all about the national election, not that it meant anything particularly to him. A man had to keep on living and working no matter who sat in the White House.

"People like us maybe don't pay much attention to things like that," Courtright said, reading his thoughts, "but these here big businessmen set a pile by who gets the job. Heard some of them say they're mighty certain we'll go to war if Lincoln wins."

Danny showed his surprise. "Pshaw!" he scoffed. "War with who? We licked the Mexicans . . ."

"War with the South," the agent said quietly. "Sure does seem trouble's brewing down there. Be a terrible thing was we to get to fightin' betwixt ourselves."

"For sure," Danny agreed. "What time in the morning do I start this run?"

"Three-thirty. You can figure on old Bob being here right on the nose. You're allowed two minutes to make the change and get going."

"Won't need it."

"Don't expect you will. And be wearing that gun. Some of the boys don't pack a weapon but you ought to on this stretch."

"Thought you said . . ."

"Ain't thinking so much about Indians. I'm just thinking you ought to go armed. Been more strangers moseying through here lately. Duded-up city fellers. Was three here only a couple of days ago. Ain't got no idea what they're up to . . . maybe nothing. But just as well you keep your eyes peeled."

"I'll do it," Danny said. He glanced about the room. "Now, if you'll point out my bunk quarters, I think I'll get me some sleep. Three-thirty comes powerful early."

"Right over there," Courtright said, waving at a door in the opposite wall. "I'll wake you for supper. You can meet the rest of the folks then."

"Fine," Danny said, rising and starting across the floor. "That'll be fine."

Excitement was having its strong way with him that next morning as he stood before the crackling fire in the rock fireplace and sipped his coffee. He was eager to be in the saddle and gone, impatient to open up this new life that lay before him. He grinned at Courtright, who winked back knowingly. Only the agent and the two hostlers were up and about at that early hour. He had met the blacksmith, his helper, the cook, and two or three other employees the evening before. Theirs were the routine jobs about the place and there was no need for them to be abroad now.

Courtright, his easy-going shape slouched in the doorway, consulted the thick, nickel-silver watch he carried. "About due," he said, and crossed to where Danny stood. "When you get going, just leave things up to the horses," he said. "They know this here route better'n any man."

Danny nodded. He finished his coffee, placed the empty cup on the mantel, and walked to the window. It was a clear night, silvered by a star-studded sky. Opening the hinged sash he listened into the deep silence. The distant, fast beat of a running horse was a faint drumming in the quiet.

"He's coming," he said, and started for the door.

"No hurry," Courtright replied, shaking his head. "Be another five, six minutes."

Danny did not pause, impatience now prodding him mercilessly. "Want to be ready," he said, and stepped out into the yard.

The station agent grinned understandingly. He reached for his sheepskin-lined jacket, drew it on. Picking up the three letters that were to be added to the mail pouch, he followed Thorpe into the brisk night. He halted where Danny was inspecting the gear on the horse readied for him by the hostlers.

"Eastern stuff," he said, thrusting the letters at Thorpe. "Goes in the right front pocket."

Danny bucked his head. Three of the compartments in the *mochila* were padlocked, contained the important mail placed in them at the beginning of the run, and could not be opened until the agent or proper official at the finish of the line — in this case St. Joe — produced the key. The fourth pocket, at the rider's right knee, was left open for pickup and delivery along the way.

Danny tucked the letters inside his shirt. He would put them in their proper pocket after he was in the saddle, not waste time doing it before he mounted. It was another of the small, seemingly insignificant things Pat McCoskey had taught him to do, all of which added together meant several minutes of time saved in the over-all run.

Satisfied his horse was ready, Danny walked deeper into the yard. The hoof beats were louder now, and, throwing his glance down the road, he caught sight of the oncoming rider.

A thrill of pride raced through him. The man was hunched forward over his mount. A scarf about his neck whipped out behind him, like some brave banner, waving its defiance to all who would see. The horse was running full tilt, head extended, mane and tail flowing in shimmering waves. His legs were no more than a blur in the semidarkness. Danny's heart bulged; this was for him — this was the sort of life he sought, must have. A man could be proud of being a Pony Express rider, and one he would be — or die trying.

The waiting horse began to pace nervously, anxious to pick up the race. One of the hostlers swore softly, affectionately, began to lead the animal about in a tight circle to relieve the tension. Suddenly the rider was thundering into the yard. Danny had a glimpse of the man's taut features as he came off his horse; he saw the oblong shape of the *mochila* as it was tossed to him. He caught it neatly, flung it over his saddle with practiced accuracy, and vaulted into place. In the next instant he was surging off into the night.

It had been a good exchange, a fast one, and Pat McCoskey would have been proud of him, he thought, as he rushed on. And then he grinned wryly. He doubted if anything would ever completely satisfy the old superintendent. To him perfection was merely a step to an even higher goal.

Jamming the three letters Wylie Courtright had given him into the *mochila*'s pocket and closing the spring snap, Danny looked ahead. The road was a faint, white ribbon curving off through a dark border of weeds, grass, and other growth. A great wave of happiness rolled through him and he took a long, deep breath of the sharp, clean air. He was in the saddle — on his way — it was real now: he was a Pony Express rider.

Or . . . almost, he thought soberly, cautioning his soaring spirits. He still must prove himself to McCoskey. He must make the run over and over again — do it right. He must heed the superintendent's instructions, remember his own oath, not forget the things Courtright had told him. He must be on time, get the mail through — and make no mistakes. It was a big order, but he would do it. Nothing must prevent his making good.

He settled lower on the saddle as the buckskin pounded on through the night. Miles fled by. Stars overhead began to pale and fade. The scraggly growth and irregular-shaped rock formations grew more distinct. A jack rabbit scurried across the road, was quickly lost in the brush. They rounded a turn and abruptly the first relay station lay before him, a small, weathered scar in the wide emptiness. It seemed hardly possible they had covered so much ground or that he had been riding for almost two hours.

He swept into the yard, the face of the hostler standing ready with his fresh mount only a soft-edged blur in the half light. Grasping the *mochila* in the manner Pat McCoskey had taught him, he prepared to make the change. It went off smoothly, without lost motion, as he had hoped, and in fleeting seconds he was again on the road, this time astride a barrel-bodied pinto gelding that ran as though all hell and its proprietor were at his heels.

An hour later, as he began to climb a long, gentle slope, sunrise caught him, bringing with it a brisk, cutting wind that struck deeply into his bones and made him wish for heavier clothing. But the wind had died by the time he made the next relay point, and, when the third change had been accomplished and without incident, he found himself unreasonably warm and removed his jacket.

Noon passed but he felt no hunger, just a gradually increasing stiffness that claimed his muscles, sent shooting pains up his back and through his shoulders. He had thought himself accustomed to hard riding, hours upon end; he was realizing now, as McCoskey had warned him, that a great difference lay between just riding a horse and forking a Pony Express mount steadily, hour after hour, at a dead run.

The country had become more desolate and the loneliness of the land began to weigh on him. He tried not to think of that, to dwell only upon the good fortune that had come his way — that would remain his if he could successfully prove his worth and ability. It was all like a dream, a vague, happy dream — one he hoped would never end.

He received a surprise near dark when he reached the final relay station, found a girl waiting with his remount. She smiled sweetly at him as he lunged past her and leaped onto the saddle. Later he could not recall whether he had smiled back or not. He would make a point of doing so on the return trip, he told himself. She had been pretty and it would be nice to know someone along the trail.

Immediately he remembered that Pony Express riders were supposed to remain unmarried, and he guessed he'd better forget about her. It could lead to problems and nothing — *nothing* — was going to interfere with his job.

It was shortly after seven-thirty when he pulled into Red Valley Station and flung the *mochila* to the waiting link rider. Every bone and muscle in his body was crying, and he staggered uncertainly as he started toward the door. He scarcely heard the greeting of the agent and shook the man's hand woodenly. He was hungry, too, but that would have to wait; first, he wanted only to stretch out on a bed for a few minutes. And then, as he passed through the doorway into the main room where an evening meal was being placed on a table for him by the agent's wife, he came to a stunned halt. Standing before the fireplace, watching him with narrowed eyes, were two men. Danny Thorpe's heart skipped a beat. It was Pete Newton and

194

Bill Stanger. Nugget Tobin's avengers had found him, after all.

Weariness dropped from Danny's shoulders, was forgotten. Worry and the old familiar feeling of hopelessness stiffened him. He stared at the pair, incongruous in the rough surroundings in their tight-fitting suits, derby hats, and button shoes.

"What do you want?"

His voice sounded strange to his own ears. It was tight, oddly husky. He watched Bill Stanger take a step forward, lift his hands, palms outward, in a conciliatory gesture.

"Want? Why, nothing, Shorty. We're just passing through, a couple of pilgrims on our way East."

"That's right," Newton chimed in. "Pilgrims, that's us."

"You're not looking for me?" Danny asked bluntly.

Stanger appeared surprised. "For you . . . oh, you mean on account of that racetrack business? Nate's done forgot that. All he wanted was to learn you a lesson. When you hightailed it, I reckon it satisfied him."

Danny considered that for several moments. It did seem unlikely Tobin would go to such lengths to even the score with him. And how could he and his thugs have known he was working for the Pony Express, or, more particularly, that he was on that exact run?

Stanger said: "How long you been carrying the mail?"

"First time out," Danny replied, and his anxiety turned to ease. Apparently the two men had no interest in him.

"Like it?"

"Real fine," Danny replied, and turned to the table. He had changed his mind; he would have something to eat before he climbed into bed.

"Beats whacking them broomtails around a track, eh?"

"Sure does," Danny said, and settled onto his chair. He raised a cup of coffee to his lips, drank gratefully. Newton spoke from across the room.

"You heading back west in the morning?"

Danny nodded. A vague doubt concerning the presence of the two men was seeping into his mind. Perhaps they were no longer interested in exacting vengeance upon him for what Tobin considered a double-cross, but there could be something else. They were much too friendly, and they were asking a lot of questions.

He puzzled over the problem while he ate, now and then casting covert glances at the pair, still standing before the fireplace. What could they be planning? The Pony Express carried little, if any, money; robbery would not be the motive, especially where a big-time gambler like Nate Tobin was involved. It had to be something else — if there were reasons for his suspicion. He finally concluded it best simply to remain quiet but keep his eyes open.

The station agent came in, sat down across the table. "Name's Ruskin. Charlie Ruskin," he said. "Didn't get much chance to introduce myself because of your friends. You'd be Danny Thorpe?"

"Right. And they're not what I'd call my friends."

Ruskin smiled, not exactly understanding. "Just figured they was from the way you were talking. Anyway, thought you'd like knowing you made the run in sixteen hours, assuming you got off on time."

"On the nose," Danny said, then added: "Is that good?"

"Just what it's figured for . . . sixteen hours. Has been done in less, and a few times when it took longer." The agent rose to his feet, a tall, friendly man with deep lines in his face. "Expect you're ready to hit the hay. First time out a rider learns he has muscles he never dreamed of."

Danny nodded, and got to his feet. "What time do I leave in the morning?"

"Six o'clock, if nothing goes wrong. Door to your left is your room. Anything you need?"

"Only sleep," Thorpe said, and moved to his quarters.

It seemed to him that he had scarcely pulled the quilts about his neck when Charlie Ruskin was shaking his shoulder.

"Five o'clock. Time you were up and around."

Danny got to his feet groggily, and then, as the sharp, cold air sliced through the fog in his brain, he dressed hurriedly and went into the lobby. He ate quickly, gulping two cups of steaming black coffee, then hastened outside to inspect his horse. The hostler had just finished saddling the animal, a half-wild little sorrel that nipped ferociously at the stableman each time he came within range.

"He's a bad one," the hostler said, "but faster'n a turpentined cat on the road. Figured that's the kind you'd be wanting."

Danny said — "What I like . . ." — then paused, realizing there was deeper meaning to the man's words. "Some reason why I ought to have a fast horse?"

The hostler glanced up. "Sure. Every rider on the line'll be pouring it on. We'll be carrying the 'lection returns."

There was pride in the man's tone. Danny grinned at him. "Danged if I hadn't forgot that!"

"Be a big feather in the company's cap, was we to get the news to Frisco in record time."

And in mine, Danny thought and walked away. The sky to the east was a dull, pearl gray. It looked like he would have good weather. He swung his eyes about the yard, back to the station. There was no sign of Pete Newton or Bill Stanger. Wondering about them, he retreated to the main room. Charlie Ruskin was at his desk.

"Nothing for you to carry on," he said, looking up. "Probably a good thing. Likely you'll be loaded."

"Probably," Danny said. "That pair . . . the ones you called my friends . . . what happened to them?"

"Rode out. About an hour ago."

"Which way?"

"Headed east, I reckon. Leastwise, that's what they said. Never paid them no mind. Why?"

He guessed he had figured them wrong. Danny sighed. Whatever it was they were up to evidently had nothing to do with him. He shrugged. "No reason. Was just asking."

He went back to the yard, crossed to where the hostler stood with the sorrel. His mind was now on the job that lay before him. He wondered if he could better the time usually required to cover the distance between the two home stations. Sixteen hours was standard, Ruskin had said. Maybe if he worked at it he could turn it down to fifteen. He would be on a good horse at the start. If he pushed him and his successive remounts hard, he just might turn the trick. A fast time record could go far in cinching the job for him.

He checked the sorrel's gear again, found it to his liking. A few minutes later the pound of hoofs announced the coming of the link rider. Tension gripping him as before, Danny took his position, made ready to receive the *mochila*, and continue the relay.

The rider entered the yard in a rush. He left his saddle in a long leap, sent the leather blanket with its bulging pockets sailing through the fading darkness at Danny.

"Lincoln won!" he shouted. "Pass it along!"

Danny spun to the sorrel, already moving out. He flung the *mochila* across the saddle, lost precious moments yanking it into position because of the fractious horse, and vaulted aboard. The sorrel was at top speed before he reached the trail.

Danny swore softly to himself. It had been a poor change over; the horse had been jumpy and too anxious. He would remember that the next time the fiery little red was given him. But actually the time loss

199

was small and the horse, seeming to know he was at fault, was doing all in his power to make up for his error. He was running hard, his hoofs beating so rapid a tattoo that the sound blended into a steady drum roll.

He gained the first relay station without the sorrel breaking stride, and he left the horse regretfully, wishing he might have him or his equal to ride the rest of the long journey. The girl was not in the yard as he made the exchange and he yelled — "Lincoln got elected!" — at the old man who stood ready with his fresh mount. The man called back — "How's that?" — but Danny was surging away and there was no time in which to repeat the news.

He was in the low-foothill country now, an area where the trail wound through a maze of bubble-like formations covered by thin brush and rock. It was the slowest section of the route, and, as the buckskin hammered his way up and down the grades and around the numberless curves, Danny saw the lead the sorrel had given him melt away.

He raised his eyes. A long slope faced him. It was one of the few straight stretches to be found in the hills and it led to a naked summit that rose several hundred feet above the surrounding land. Beyond it, he recalled, lay a wide swale. Once over the rim the buckskin could do better.

Suddenly the horse paused in stride. Danny saw first a puff of white smoke off to the side of the road. Then came the dry slap of a gunshot. The buckskin's head went down, then snapped up as his legs folded beneath him. Danny felt himself soaring through space.

Abruptly the ground came up and met him with solid, sickening force.

He fought his way back to consciousness slowly. His head ached and there was a stabbing pain in his left shoulder. He became aware of voices and opened his eyes. He lay full length in a sandy wash a few yards from the road. The luckless buckskin, dead, was just beyond. The *mochila*, the contents of its unlocked pocket strewn about, was close by. A newspaper, unfolded, its bold black headlines proclaiming the election of Abraham Lincoln to the Presidency, had been examined and tossed aside.

"How long you stalling around here?"

Danny started. Pete Newton's voice! Ignoring the pain that raced through him, he twisted about to where he could see better. The two men were a dozen paces to his right. They had shed their city clothing, were now dressed for hard riding. Newton was tightening the cinch of his saddle.

"Not long. Got to get rid of him and that mail. Then I'll be coming."

Newton hesitated. "Could lend you a hand."

"Better not take the time. Sooner we get the word passed to Nate, the better. Shape that nag of mine's in, I'd slow you down, anyway."

Pete Newton finished his chore, swung onto his horse. "Maybe you ought to just leave things as they are. Ain't so sure it's smart to go fooling around with the U.S. mail . . ."

Stanger swore impatiently. "Quit fretting about it! Let me take care of my end. You get the word to Tobin. He stands to make a pile of cash on this deal and I sure wouldn't want to be the one who knocked him out of it."

Newton muttered something and pulled his horse about, headed for the road. "So long!" he called back over his shoulder. Stanger only nodded.

Understanding came quickly to Danny Thorpe. Tobin was gambling heavily on the election. By knowing the results in advance and also delaying the delivery of that information, he stood to make a fortune. Stanger and Newton had been dispatched to accomplish that end.

A hopelessness settled over Danny as frustration gripped him. Why did it have to happen to him? Why did Tobin's thugs have to choose the very run he was on? Was it because he was a green rider on the job? Or was it that such things always seemed to come his way?

That was it, he concluded bitterly. That — and the fact that the run he was on was the longest, most forsaken and desolate stretch in the entire line. Such made it easy for them to work their plan. *Let something go haywire . . . and it'll end up in my lap*, he moaned to himself.

Through despairing eyes he watched Newton strike off westward. Stanger, too, kept his gaze on the departing man for a time, then turned, walked leisurely toward Danny. His jaw was set and his hand rested on the butt of the pistol hanging at his hip. Danny felt his throat tighten. He would have no chance against a killer such as Bill Stanger; all he could do was lie still, feign unconsciousness. Maybe something would turn up — a bit of good luck . . .

Luck! The word caught in Danny Thorpe's mind, began to glow vividly. What was it old Pat McCoskey had said? *A man makes his own luck.* It was true, he realized. It was wrong just to sit back, take what fate threw at him — and not fight. When a man fought for his rights, he changed things, made them go his way. Maybe he failed in the trying, maybe he even died — but at least he'd had a hand in his own destiny.

A hard core of denial, of brittle resentment, began to build within Danny Thorpe. He still had his pistol. Bill Stanger and Pete Newton held him in such low esteem they had not bothered to remove it. But it was under him and he could not reach it without moving. He dared not do that. Let Stanger think him still unconscious; against a killer like him it was necessary to lesson the odds in some way.

Stanger halted a step to his left, a tower of intimidation staring down at the small man. Danny could feel his cold eyes drilling into the back of his head. Stanger was considering his next move. Danny waited, utterly motionless. After an eternity Stanger turned, walked to where the opened newspaper lay, something apparently capturing his attention.

Danny gathered his strength. He must act now or forever be lost. Ignoring the pain in his shoulder, he came to a crouching position, drew his weapon. Stanger was still reading, his back partly turned. A faint

203

dizziness swept through Danny, and then a sudden wave of doubt. He brushed both away, sprang upright.

At the sound of crunching sand Stanger whirled. His mouth dropped open in surprise, then hardened. A broad, patronizing grin spread over his dark face.

"Now, Shorty, you know you're too little to go messing around with a gun," he said in a dry, sarcastic voice. "Better you drop it," he added, and reached for his own weapon.

Danny fired once. Stanger jolted as the bullet smashed into his chest. Again surprise blanked his features. He frowned and abruptly caved in, went full length onto the warming sand.

Danny wasted no time checking the effect of his single bullet. He spun, dropped to his knees beside the *mochila*. Scooping up the spilled mail, he crammed it into its pocket, snapped the flap into place. Rising, he ran to Stanger's horse, threw the leather blanket into position, and mounted. Spurring the long-legged bay roughly, he got him back to the road and struck out hard for the next relay station.

The bay should last that far, he reasoned, rubbing at his throbbing shoulder. Then, with a fresh horse, he would have a good chance of overtaking Pete Newton. He had lost a good half hour, possibly more, so he could forget his hopes of making a record run. But he would get the mail through.

The bay began to tire after the first five miles of steady running. Danny slacked up on the reins. It would be folly to run the horse into the ground. He must nurse the brute along, keep him going even if it resolved into a slow trot. Anything would be faster than being on foot.

He wondered if Pete Newton's horse was in the same condition, guessed it likely was. A new thought entered his mind. Tobin had probably set up a relay of his own. Courtright had mentioned three strangers. Two of them would have been Stanger and Newton. The third was likely stationed somewhere farther along the route — and, if that was true, then there would be others strung out all the way to San Francisco. Overtaking and halting Newton loomed more important to Danny Thorpe at that realization.

He reached the relay point with the bay near exhaustion. The hostler stared at him as he came off the saddle and leaped onto his remount.

"You're late!" the man shouted.

Danny shook his head, called back — "Lincoln won!" — and raced on down the road.

He felt better now with a fresh horse under him. He wished there had been time enough to inquire about Newton, ask the hostler if he had noted a passing rider, but he could not afford the delay. Arriving so far behind schedule was going to be a mark against him, could even place his hopes for permanent assignment in jeopardy. It was best he recover all the time possible. He would see Pete Newton soon enough. The sorrel he now rode was covering the ground with amazing speed — or else it seemed so after the slow grind on Stanger's worn bay.

He caught a glimpse of Tobin's man a half hour later. Newton was topping a rise a quarter mile distant. He heard the beat of the sorrel and Danny watched him twist about, could visualize the surprise that would cover his face.

Immediately Newton began to flog his horse, moving then at an easy gallop. Danny considered the man's frantic efforts to pull away, at least to maintain his lead. But his mount was no match for the fresh sorrel. The gap closed rapidly. When no more than a hundred yards separated them, Newton resorted to his pistol and began to shoot. Danny had hoped it would not come to gun play; the shock of having killed Bill Stranger was still a heavy sickness within him. Yet he knew deeply in his mind that it was useless to hope; men such as Newton and Stanger recognized no other solution when cornered.

He drew his own weapon, bided his time. The distance between them was still too great for a handgun. The sorrel thundered on. The spread decreased. Newton, reloading, opened up again. Danny heard the angry *whirr* of bullets. He was near enough. He leveled off on Newton, aiming for the man's shoulder, squeezed the trigger twice. Newton bucked on his saddle, heaved to one side. Immediately his horse slowed, began to veer away. Newton's gun fell to the ground, sending up a spurt of dry dust when it struck. The horse stopped. Newton folded, clung to the saddle horn.

Danny, not slackening his speed, drew abreast. He threw a searching glance at the man, saw that he was only wounded. He sighed in relief, shouted — "I'll send somebody back for you!" — and rushed on.

He was feeling better now. He had halted Tobin's makeshift relay, checked his scheme to fleece a lot of people — a scheme in which the Pony Express had been an innocent participant. And he had won over himself. He smiled grimly at that thought; yes, he had won the battle — but likely he had lost the war.

He swept into the next relay station, paused only long enough to shout instructions concerning Pete Newton, and then hurried on determined to make up as much lost time as possible. But a mile is a mile and a horse can do only so much. When he rode into Smith's Crossing late that night, he knew he was nearly an hour behind schedule.

Weary, dejected, expecting the worst, he entered the station. Explanations would mean nothing; they would sound like alibis. To be sure, he could produce the reason for his delay. He could have Newton brought in, but Newton, of course, would deny everything — as would Nate Tobin. And Stanger was dead. It would help little anyway. Other Pony Express riders had such problems, dealt with them, and still managed to maintain their schedules. It was a part of the job and expected of them.

"Running a mite behind, ain't you, boy?"

Pat McCoskey's raspy voice cut him like a whip. He hauled up sharply, stared at the superintendent while his spirits sagged lower. McCoskey had ridden out to check on him, to see what sort of a job he was doing. On that he would base his decision as to whether Danny Thorpe became a permanent employee or not.

"Afraid I am," Danny said miserably. "Sorry about it."

"Sorry!" McCoskey rumbled. "What you being sorry for? Far as I'm concerned, you done fine. New men generally get all fired up trying to impress everybody about how good they are. Do their best to make the run faster'n it ever been done before. Glad to see you ain't that kind. Shows you'll make a good rider."

Danny's eyes filled with disbelief. A grin cracked his lips. Then he sobered. He had to be honest about it. "Yes, sir, but I was . . . ," he began, and then checked his words as Wylie Courtright frowned, shook his head meaningfully at him.

"Time average was real good," the station agent said, stepping up to McCoskey's side. "Figures out a little more than sixteen and a half hours each way. And you had a heavy *mochila*. Can't ask for much better from a new man."

"And I ain't," McCoskey added, smiling, something he was seldom guilty of. "Hope you like it here with Wylie, son. It's going to be your regular station."

Danny could only bob his head happily. Something was blocking his throat, choking him, causing his heart to sing with a new joy he had never known. He couldn't put it into words even to himself, but a wonderful thing had happened. Danny Thorpe had at last found himself and his place.

Truth at Gunpoint

Rome Bellman stood quietly in the darkness of the oak thicket. The others had not come yet, and except for his bay horse he was completely alone as he waited, absently listening to the muted, mysterious noises of the night that were all around him. A lean and angular man, his face bore a studied gravity, as if his eyes had seen too much of life's bitter side, too little of its kindness, and, as he stood there rigidly in the shadowy depth of the trees, feeble starlight touched him gently, lent an unreal quality to his being.

But such was a false impression. Rome Bellman was a hard, practical man, burnished and browned by the endless hours of working his range, nursing a herd of cattle that increased with aggravating slowness, protecting it while still coping with the every day problems of life itself.

Somewhere, far down in the valley that spread out below him like a vast, deep-shaded carpet, a dog barked, and he stirred, turned that way. The sound reached into him, brought his thoughts into motion, and took him back to his own ranch beyond the ridge, to what it represented — and to his wife Sara.

A sigh slipped from his long lips as he ran a hand over his bare head. Women sometimes just could not understand. Like this matter of tonight — but maybe after it was all over, he would be able to make her see that he was right. After all, a man had obligations and must live by his conscience — do what he thought right and best.

He dug into his shirt pocket, dug out the thick, nickeled watch that had been his father's, glanced at the face. The men — other small ranchers such as himself — should be showing up by this time: Charlie Dearing, who always came first; Ben Stanhope whose place was near the creek; Courtney Swayne; Pearl Middlemarch from the valley to the north; and Tennessee Jordan whose spread adjoined his.

Shortly he heard the humus-deadened approach of a horse coming in on the north edge of the grove and turned that way. The rider came into view, swung in, and halted. Rome saw that it was Jordan, and he had a moment's wonder about Dearing.

Jordan, accent blurring the edges of his words, said: "Am I late?"

Bellman, match light flaring yellow against the taut skin of his face as he lit the smoke he had just rolled, shook his head: "Thought you were Dearing."

"He not here yet? Odd . . ."

"What I was thinking."

The men fell silent for a time, and then Tennessee Jordan spoke again: "Could be he's sick . . . or mayhaps he's having himself a bit of wife trouble . . . Old woman of mine's sure on the warpath."

"Know what you mean," Rome said, not smiling, and remembered Sara's words and the stiff, still way she had looked when she had said them.

"Yours, too?"

The tall rancher sighed, nodded. "Just some things you can't make a woman understand . . . like the importance of only two or three steers to a man when he's getting started."

"For a fact. Tried to tell my old woman that this was something we had to do. She kept throwing it up to me that we've got a sheriff in town now and it was his job and we ought to be letting him do it."

Bellman nodded again, blew a thin cloud of smoke into the cool night, hearing familiar things. He started to make some reply, hesitated as the sound of more riders came to them. A bit later Middlemarch and Stanhope rode in. Before they could dismount, McAuliffe and Swayne arrived and all dropped to the ground, stood about in a quiet, subdued group, exchanging their greetings, making brief comments, and having their wonder about Charlie Dearing, too.

At half past eight o'clock Rome Bellman said: "No use waiting. He won't be coming."

They turned to their horses and stepped into the saddle, each man taking a mask from his pocket and pulling it over his head.

"You reckon this'll be the last time?" McAuliffe said to Bellman.

"Could be, Henry," Rome answered as they moved out of the trees at a slow walk and headed for town and the saloon where Gar Morgan and his bunch hung out.

211

As they traveled, Rome Bellman was thinking of
Charlie Dearing, and of the things Tennessee Jordan
had said, and of the way Sara had looked at him when
he left the house. And he was remembering how it
started with them — over a week ago — when the new
sheriff, Clee Endicott, had paid them a call.

Endicott, a slim, dark man with deliberate ways that
matched his cool eyes, had said: "Bellman, I don't
know if you're one of the vigilantes or not. My hunch is
you are, but one thing sure . . . you know them. What I
want understood is that I'm the law in this country
now, and I don't need help. If ever I do, I'll sing out for
it."

Rome had answered: "One man can't control this
country . . . and rustling's getting worse."

"Know that, but it's up to the law to stop it, not a
bunch of masked riders. If you or anybody else will
bring me the proof I'm looking for, I'll put a stop to the
thieving."

"Gar Morgan's behind it . . . you know that."

"Maybe I do, but I've got to have proof before I can
act."

"My point," Bellman had said then. "It's the way the
law works . . . and a man could go broke waiting on it
to do something. Leaves it up to him and his neighbors
to do what has to be done, make a stand against the
likes of Morgan . . ."

"Leave Gar Morgan to me," Endicott had cut in.
"Just tell the vigilantes to forget their masked riding
and tend to their ranching."

212

"Nothing they'd like more . . . and it's something they'll surer'n hell do when the time comes and they can. But it ain't here now. One-man law won't work."

"It's working now . . . and the vigilantes had best stay out of it," the sheriff had said, turning to his horse. "You pass that warning along . . . they're to leave the law to me."

Afterward Sara had said to him: "It is his job, Rome. You will tell the others?"

He had shaken his head. "I can't. The country's not ready for his kind of law yet."

She had drawn away from him, and, looking at her, he had read her thoughts and known that something dark and strong was rising between them. "*You* can't," she had murmured, "but you can ride off into the night leaving me to worry, to wonder if I'll ever see you alive again while you and the others are going about your vengeance."

"It is not a matter of vengeance . . . only of keeping the law."

"Whatever, it is no longer something that you must do. I have worried myself sick for the last time, Rome."

"Jordan . . . McAuliffe, the others . . . they take their chances, too, knowing it must be done."

"I don't care about the others, only about my own husband," Sara had replied, standing very straight. "You talk of obligations . . . have you none to me?"

At once he had said: "You know that I do . . . that you are a part of that obligation." He had stopped there, stood quietly, letting his gaze drift out over the sun-flooded land. It was a good country, a fine place to build a life, but there was a price, and, if a man would stay, he must meet that cost. "Once the Morgan bunch is gone, likely there'll be no more trouble, and . . ."

"There'll be others!" she had said bitterly. "Rome . . . if you go, I won't be here when you get back . . . if you do."

That had turned him silent, and then some of his hard pride had boiled to the surface and he had said in a flat voice: "A wife should try to understand what her husband must do . . . but if that is the way it is . . . so be it," and had gone on out to the corral where he had work to do. Later, when the appointed evening had arrived, he had strapped on his big hog-leg of a revolver, mounted the bay gelding, and ridden away without looking back.

Now, as he led the small party down the narrow side valley that would take them to the settlement by a round-about route, he was recalling his own words and remembering the stricken look in Sara's eyes when he had voiced them and there was for him a measure of doubt as to whether being right had much worth.

He wondered, too, if the others were having like thoughts as they followed him, if they, also, had gone through moments of indecision and perhaps had been faced with a problem such as his. If so, then like him, they had placed their obligations and duty first, their personal needs second, and were there, riding with him. All, that is, but Charlie Dearing, and in that man's absence Bellman wondered if he was not reading the signs of what was to come.

As time wore on and the masked committee was required to continue its operation, there likely would be others who would not put in an appearance, influenced by one reason or another, and perhaps, one day, he would stand alone. It would matter little — he would continue alone if he deemed it necessary, for that was the way Rome Bellman was cut — a man sure of purpose, definite in mind, and ready to face any odds if he knew he was right.

Star shine filled the valley with a dull-silver glow and spread out like a pale sheet across the flats. A coyote flung his challenge against them as they topped the last ridge and started down the long grade that led to the settlement, lying in a shallow swale hard by Medicine Creek. When they reached the first of the sun-grayed buildings, Bellman lifted his hand, and they halted.

Most of the stores were dark, as they had expected, but at the yonder end of the single street where the Bonanza Saloon sprawled apart and to itself there was light and the faint tinkle of a piano mixing with the sound of laughter and voices. There was no life within the newly furnished office of the sheriff, but the door was open and Rome had a moment's wonder if the lawman was inside, sitting in the blackness. It did not matter.

"We'll stay to the alley," he said, swinging off the roadway, and the others followed him and the bay at a quiet walk to the rear of the Bonanza. In that interval each checked his mask, inspected his weapon while a throbbing tension built itself within them.

Reaching the desired point, Bellman motioned for a halt, and slid from the saddle. Excitement raveled along his nerves as he moved silently to a side window in the building and stood there, searching out the room, noting carefully those who stood at the bar, those who were at the tables and those who simply lounged against the walls. Finally he returned, went back onto his saddle.

"Two missing," he said. "We should wait a while."

Wordlessly they merged back into the shadows some yards distant from the structure where they could command a view of the building's front and rear entrances, and there began their vigil, no man speaking. Minutes dragged by, long and filled only with the sounds of the off-key piano, the laugh of a woman somewhere back along the street.

A man appeared, emerging from one of the lesser saloons, made his way to the Bonanza, and entered.

"That's one," Tennessee Jordan said. "I'm remembering him . . . Rides a buckskin."

McAuliffe sighed deeply. "Good. Who's still missing, Rome?"

"The red-headed one . . ."

"Figure he's important enough to hold back for? They all might take the notion to pull out . . . and this setting around is honing me to an edge."

Bellman considered, said — "All right, let's go then." — and came off the bay.

They led their horses to the rack and moved in Indian file along the side of the Bonanza to its front. Pausing there, they adjusted their masks, drew their

216

pistols. Bellman glanced about, assured himself that all were ready, and then laid a hand against one of the batwings.

"Let's have done with it," he said, and pushed back the door, and stepped inside. With the others quickly following, fanning out on either side, he proceeded a quarter of the way into the smoke-filled building.

Talk cut instantly and a dozen faces turned to them in surprise. The bartender set a bottle he was holding down carefully, leaned against the bar, ironic amusement crossing his features.

Bellman, his eyes on Gar Morgan and the men who ran with him, slouched in chairs around a table near the center of the room. Morgan raised his hands above his head.

"Nobody makes a move . . . then nobody will get hurt. We're here for one man . . . Morgan."

The outlaw rose lazily from his chair, head slung forward, glanced about the saloon. He grinned. "You was a long time coming."

"When we do, we're sure. Put your hands on your hat and walk toward us."

Again Morgan smiled. "Mister, I ain't about to accommodate you. You want me, you'll just have to walk over here and get me . . . which is sure liable to turn out to be a chore for you."

"Make it easy on yourself," Bellman said. "Shooting you down here's not much different from stringing you up to a tree. Both get done what's needful."

Tension was mounting higher in the murky room. Rome could feel it, could see it in the faces of the men ranged along the bar and hunched around the tables. It was risky to let things ride. Someone was bound to make a wrong move and some innocent bystander could get hurt.

"Seems you've had yourself a trial over me and got your verdict already in," Morgan said.

"Right. We traced twenty head of rustled cattle to you through the man you sold them to. Been more, but that one time's all we needed. Expect we could prove you had a hand in robbing the Denver stage and burning down the way station, too, was it necessary."

Morgan laughed, glanced around at the men at the table. "Hear that, boys? Seems we got us somebody that's really keeping track of us. Just didn't come to my mind that we was all that popular!"

Rome listened to the laughter, eyes touching the men around Morgan. There were only four of his regulars with him — yet earlier, when he had looked through the window, all had been present except two. Now three were missing.

"Tell you what, Mister Vigilante" — Morgan smiled sardonically — "I'll just save you some bothering . . . me and my boys done all them things you claim, and a few more besides, and we don't give a good hooting god damn who knows it! Now, what do you think of that?"

Beneath his mask Rome felt a rush of anger at the outlaw's brazen admission of his crimes. This was the reason why he and men like Jordan and McAuliffe and the others still had to ride the hills and weed out the unwanted. And until all of the Morgans and their kind

218

were wiped out, no man and his family could expect to lead a peaceful and decent life.

"Your last chance, Morgan. Either you're coming or . . ."

"You ain't told us yet," the outlaw cut in, seemingly enjoying the moments greatly, "what about my boys? You aiming to string them up, too?"

"We'll get to them. You come first on the list. If they're still around when we're done with you, then they can figure on hearing from us, too."

"Well, that's plenty nice of you, but happens I got a different idea about things. We're going to hold us a little trial right here . . . me and my boys. We're going to try *you*, and" — Morgan paused, swept the room with his arrogant glance — "any of you who don't exactly agree with what we decide had best keep his trap shut. That clear?"

There was no reply from the bystanders. Morgan resumed his easy, bantering manner, placed his attention upon Bellman and the men flanking him once more.

"Now, if you'll just sort of turn around, easy like, maybe you'll see what I'm talking about."

Rome, suddenly taut as realization came to him, twisted about, looked over his shoulder. The three missing outlaws — they had come in from behind, were lined up across the doorway, guns in hand, grinning wickedly.

McAuliffe swore softly. Swayne lowered his weapon, shrugged as if recognizing a moment that had come at last. The rest remained frozen. Bellman, his nerves

219

stringing out to wire tightness, gave his own carelessness a bitter thought, swung back to the outlaw chief. He could blame no one but himself for this; he had allowed his personal problems to fill his mind, prevent his thinking clearly.

"You'll not get by with this," he said. "There'll be others who'll come . . . fight you . . ."

"Ain't likely," Morgan said dryly. "Lot of sheep in most men . . . and they won't want trouble from me. Now, you all just stand easy while one of my . . . my deputies . . . passes between you and collects your hardware. Don't hardly seem right for prisoners about to get themselves hung should have guns in their hands."

Rome Bellman drew himself up stiffly. Here and now in this smoke-filled saloon the future of the valley would be settled. There was no choice, and, if it cost him his life taking that of Gar Morgan, then, at least, he would have paid his dues, and families like his own — wives like Sara would be able to live in peace.

Maybe Tennessee and Stanhope and McAuliffe and Swayne and Middlemarch and himself, paying with their blood, would establish once and for all the one-man law that Clee Endicott represented. Not turning, he allowed his shoulders to draw back, the long-ago agreed upon signal to the others that the moment of violence was at hand. All would drop to their knees when the fingers of his left hand clenched, and the shooting would begin.

One of Morgan's men pulled away from the table, started toward them, swaggering, grinning. In the absolute hush that lay over the room, the strike of his heels on the bare floor was like a measured drumbeat.

Rome, giving Sara a final, regretful thought, steeled himself, allowed his left arm to ease forward. He began to close his fingers. The hard voice of Clee Endicott, rapping across the silence, stopped him.

"Far enough! Any man that moves . . . is dead!"

Bellman threw his glance to the source of the words. The lawman had come in from the rear door, was standing at the end of the narrow hall that led into the main part of the saloon. A cocked six-gun was in each of his hands, the muzzles drifting slowly back and forth, covering everyone.

"Morgan . . . I heard enough to put you and your bunch away for a long spell. I'm arresting all of you. Keep your hands up where I can see them . . . high."

Relief running through him, Rome started to move across to the lawman. Endicott's voice slapped at him.

"Don't move . . . vigilante! Far as I'm concerned any man wearing a rag over his face is an outlaw, too."

Bellman settled back on his heels. No one had stirred except him. Morgan, the hardcases at the table with him, the three outlaws who had slipped through the batwings, to spring the trap — all were rooted to the spot, pinned motionlessly by one man wearing a star. Suddenly the truth, like a shaft of light, broke through to Rome Bellman; the law, by the very fact that it was the law, had the strength of many.

"Take off them masks!"

Using his free hand, Rome pulled the cloth from his head, dropped it on the floor. Jordan and the others followed his example.

"Told you once," Endicott said, "was I ever to need help doing my job, I'd ask for it. I'm asking now . . . a lawman calling on decent citizens to step in, to uphold the law. Do I make myself clear?"

Rome Bellman nodded. Murmurs of agreement came from the men near him as they trained their weapons on the outlaws.

"I'm saying *decent* citizens . . . not masked riders," Endicott continued pointedly. "Want that understood now . . . and from here on."

Bellman moved his head slightly. "The meaning's plain, Sheriff," he said, and, kicking the pile of masks into a nearby corner, stepped to the lawman's side. "Call on us anytime."

He was sure Sara would approve that sort of an arrangement.

About the Author

Ray Hogan was an author who inspired a loyal following over the years since he published his first Western novel, *Ex-Marshal*, in 1956. Hogan was born in Willow Springs, Missouri, where his father was town marshal. At five the Hogan family moved to Albuquerque where they lived in the foothills of the Sandia and Manzano mountains. His father was on the Albuquerque police force and, in later years, owned the Overland Hotel. It was while listening to his father and other old-timers tell tales from the past that Ray was inspired to recast these tales in fiction. From the beginning he did exhaustive research into the history and the people of the Old West, and the walls of his study were lined with various firearms, spurs, pictures, books, and memorabilia, about all of which he could talk in dramatic detail. "I've attempted to capture the courage and bravery of those men and women that lived out West and the dangers and problems they had to overcome," Hogan once remarked. If his lawmen protagonists seem sometimes larger than life, it is because they are men of integrity, heroes who through grit of character and common sense are able to overcome the obstacles they encounter despite often overwhelming odds. This same grit of character can also be found in Hogan's heroines, and in *The Vengeance of Fortuna West* (1983) Hogan wrote a gripping and totally believable account of a woman who takes up the badge and tracks the men who killed her lawman husband by ambush. No less intriguing in her way is Nellie Dupray, convicted of rustling in *The Glory Trail* (1978). One of his most popular books, dealing with an earlier period in the West with Kit Carson as its protagonist, is *Soldier in Buckskin* (Five Star Westerns, 1996). Above all, what is most impressive about Hogan's Western novels is the consistent quality with which each is crafted, the compelling depth of his characters, and his ability to juxtapose the complexities of human conflict into narratives always as intensely interesting as they are emotionally involving.